continued . . .

FRINGE GIRL in Love

Valerie Frankel

nal JAM books

NAL Jam

Published by New American Library, a division of
Penguin Group (USA) Inc., 375 Hudson Street, New York, New York 10014, USA
Penguin Group (Canada), 90 Eglinton Avenue East, Suite 700, Toronto,
Ontario M4P 2Y3, Canada (a division of Pearson Penguin Canada Inc.)
Penguin Books Ltd., 80 Strand, London WC2R 0RL, England
Penguin Ireland, 25 St. Stephen's Green, Dublin 2, Ireland (a division of Penguin Books Ltd.)
Penguin Group (Australia), 250 Camberwell Road, Camberwell, Victoria 3124,
Australia (a division of Pearson Australia Group Pty. Ltd.)
Penguin Books India Pvt. Ltd., 11 Community Centre, Panchsheel Park, New Delhi – 110 017, India
Penguin Group (NZ), 67 Apollo Drive, Mairangi Bay,
Auckland 1311, New Zealand (a division of Pearson New Zealand Ltd.)
Penguin Books (South Africa) (Pty.) Ltd., 24 Sturdee Avenue,
Rosebank, Johannesburg 2196, South Africa

Penguin Books Ltd., Registered Offices:
80 Strand, London WC2R 0RL, England

First published by NAL Jam, an imprint of New American Library,
a division of Penguin Group (USA) Inc.

First Printing, April 2007
1 3 5 7 9 10 8 6 4 2

NAL JAM and logo are trademarks of Penguin Group (USA) Inc.

LIBRARY OF CONGRESS CATALOGING-IN-PUBLICATION DATA:
Frankel, Valerie.
Fringe girl in love / Valerie Frankel.
p. cm.
Summary: As she learns about tragic love stories in English literature, sixteen-year-old Dora experi-
ences her own romantic misery with boyfriend Noel and witnesses the fracturing and mending of
relationships of those close to her at home and at her exclusive Brooklyn private school.
ISBN-13: 978-0-451-22046-2
ISBN-10: 0-451-22046-3
[1. Interpersonal relations—Fiction. 2. Love—Fiction. 3. Schools—Fiction.] I. Title.
PZ7.F8553Fm 2007
[Fic]—dc22   2006026105

Set in Bembo
Designed by Spring Hoteling

Printed in the United States of America

Dedicated to The Little Sisters Club

One

So far this school year, I'd had three boyfriends, started a student revolution, lost and regained my two best friends. I thought the rest of my junior year would run smoothly in comparison to its bumpy beginning. Turned out (and this shouldn't have surprised me, given my track record) I was wrong.

From where I stood now, at the kitchen window of my apartment, the second semester looked fresh and clean, a snowy white slate. January always felt like a brand-spanking-new start. And I was just over the edge of seventeen; my birthday was a few weeks ago. Should everything proceed according to plan, I would lose it ("it" being exactly what one would assume) this year. Part of my age-of-consent agenda was to boldly go where I had never gone before.

A Monday-morning blanket of the fluffy white stuff

covered the sidewalks. Little piles of snow perched precarious-ly in tree branches. Through the window, I watched fat flakes fall and stick. I sipped my coffee, enjoyed the silence, felt poetic and melancholic, imagined myself a portrait of peace and con-templation. The moment passed when my parents flounced downstairs in their matching his-and-her chenille bathrobes. They were holding hands and sneaking secret smiles, which were about as subtle as a flashing neon beer sign.

Joya, my younger sister, beamed at them and said, "Good morning!" She happily munched her toast and jam. Her eyes shone with pure, unadulterated love for our parents. Joya was in eighth grade, old enough to know what Mom and Dad's disgusting lovey-dovey signals meant. But Joya didn't pick up other people's signals. She tuned in to a magical frequency of her own—one that only she, her boyfriend Ben, dolphins, unicorns and zombies could hear.

Mom kissed Joya on the top of her precious pixie-ish head. "It is a beautiful day, isn't it?" asked Mom, her voice way too singsongy for seven thirty a.m.

She dared to flounce in my direction, actually came at me with outstretched arms. "Don't even think about it," I warned.

"Eggs?" asked my dad. "Waffles? Is there anyone in this room who wants bacon?"

"I do!" said Joya.

"I do!" said Mom, eyes twinkling. "I'm absolutely *starving* this morning."

Dad smiled (slyly, nauseatingly) and said, "Me, too. Famished."

They giggled.

I gagged.

Joya asked, "Dora, are you okay?"

"I've got to go," I said.

As per our custom, Eli and Liza (my two best friends) were meeting me before the start of the second semester at Grind, a café on Montague Street. Our aim: to regroup and plot the upcoming trimester at the Brownstone Collegiate Institute, our private school in Brooklyn Heights, New York. I put on my coat, hat, scarf, gloves and backpack, and trudged out the door before (1) Joya could ask to tag along, (2) Mom offered me unwanted advice or (3) Dad forced pork product on me.

"My parents have reached a point of frightening transparency," I announced to Eli and Liza at Grind while sipping my pumpkin spice latte. "They're writing a new book, *His-and-Her Romance*, taking their own advice way too literally."

Eli and Liza nodded sympathetically. We were smug in our own romances these days. All of us had boyfriends at the same time (a pivotal first). And we were riding the crest of a friendship wave, too. Incredible to think that two months ago, I was a friendless, boyfriendless, pathetic loser, hanging my head in shame and regret. Now I had the rich, textured, slamming social life of a girl in a shampoo commercial.

Turned on a frigging dime—life. That was what I was afraid of.

"I don't like to see Mom and Dad—or anyone—too happy," I said. "Makes you worry."

"Makes *you* worry," said Eli Stomp, dabbing her red lips with a napkin. Only she, with her tidy black sweater set, pin-straight Chinese hair and unblemished porcelain skin, could make quaffing coffee seem dainty.

"I get what Dora means," said Liza Greene, a strand of blond hair dipping accidentally into her cup as she drank lusti-ly from it. "You don't want to tempt fate." Despite her carefree urban hippie style, Liza was the most anxious and superstitious of our threesome.

"Eventually something bad is bound to happen," said Eli pragmatically. "But then you just deal with it."

"Sometimes a situation is beyond your control," said Liza.

I assumed she was referring to her mother Stephanie's im-minent wedding to Gary "the Whitest Man on Earth" Glitch. Since I'd listened to Liza moan about the dreaded upcoming nuptials every day for hours at a stretch (time I could have spent playing Snood or probing my beloved Noel Kepner's dental work with my tongue), I steered the conversation in another direction.

"Ms. Barbaloo needs hip replacement," I informed the table. "She's taking a medical tourism vacation to Thailand to have surgery and convalesce. Should be *months* before she comes back to Brownstone." I spoke of an older-than-bedrock, blue-haired, notoriously strict upper school English teacher.

"My dad said hip replacement is an absolutely gruesome surgery," said Eli, a doctor's daughter. "They have to use a circular saw and cut through the bones of Ms. Barbaloo's pelvis."

"Nice sound effects," said Liza of Eli's violent whirring.

"Can you not use 'Ms. Barbaloo' and 'pelvis' in the same sentence ever again?" I asked. "The substitute English professor arrives today from some WASPy prep school in New England. She is, allegedly, a Shakespearean scholar."

"I think Ms. Barbaloo might have met Shakespeare in her youth," said Eli.

" 'Love Stories in English Literature,' " said Liza, who was in the class with me, as well as her boyfriend, Stanley Nable, and mine, Noel Kepner. She added, "New teacher. Sexy stories. Should be a decent class."

I was counting on it. The rest of my course load veered from deadly to fatal. Ideally, English class would be the romantic antidote to my otherwise necromantic schedule. The love theme would play nicely into my personal schedule, too. English was the only hour (besides lunch) I would spend at Brownstone with Noel this term. As for out of school, I pictured us reading the required passages to each other on the bed in my room, lava lamp light flickering across our faces, open books on our laps. When we leaned close to kiss, the volumes would slide off, hitting the floor with twin thuds.

"Too freaking hot!" said Eli suddenly. "Why do they crank the radiators in here? I can feel the moisture being sucked out of my pores." She gathered her stuff. "I told Eric I'd meet him before class at the *Brief* office." Her boyfriend, Eric Brainard, was editor of the student-published broadsheet.

I checked my watch. How time flew when consuming ridiculous amounts of coffee and cookies.

The three of us walked the four blocks to Brownstone. The snow had tapered off and was now only dandrufflike flakes. The sidewalks on Montague Street had been salted. We passed Tandoori Palace, Souvlaki Hut, Sushi Den, Pagoda House, Caffe Amoure and Burger Heaven. One could circle the globe cuisine-wise on one block in Brooklyn Heights. Or, if you wanted to stay home, the world delivered.

"I hate winter," I said as we walked. And I did. I was supersensitive to cold. Always had been. But, if I thought I'd been chilly on the walk to school, my blood froze solid when we got there. On the steps leading up to Brownstone's arched front doorway, Noel Kepner, my dear heart, had his arm around the shoulder of Sondra Fortune, my sworn enemy (or lifelong friend—our relationship was a massive gray area). He was laughing at something she'd said. Sondra and Noel used to go out, and not a million years ago.

My mood-indicator hazel eyes changed color, from placid gray to roiling, boiling green—the color of jealousy that was nearly impossible to see through. But Noel saw me. He waved in his eager, earnest way. His smile was genuine, big, lovable, and it defused my jealous rage somewhat. But not enough. As far as Sondra went . . . then again, Sondra never went as far as I wanted her to. I'd like to see her relocate to the moon.

At my side, Eli said, "Steady, Dora."

I ascended the steps, my jaw locked. Noel pulled me into a hug and kissed me—on the forehead. Cute. When he let me go, Sondra was gone. So were Eli and Liza.

He said, "You smell like pumpkin."

I said, "Noel, since you're my boyfriend, I'd like you to do one small thing for me—not to prove your love but to acknowledge a flaw in my character, a charming flaw, a lovable quirk."

"What's that?" he asked, smiling.

"Don't touch other girls." Especially that one.

"Sondra is my friend, Dora," he said. "I've known her since we were seven."

"You've known me since we were five," I said. "You've had sex with her, so she'll always be more than a friend." I didn't bother reminding him that we had yet to permanently change the status of our friendship. Noel knew only too well that that we hadn't crossed that Rubicon. In a way, our doing it would be like buying off the sale rack: There would be no return once the purchase was made. You were stuck, in more ways than one.

I loved Noel. I trusted him. I felt we were drawing ever closer. To "it." But when I saw him touch Sondra Fortune—even on the padded shoulder of her down jacket—it was like I didn't know him, didn't trust him, wanted nothing to do with him.

"Come on," he said, throwing an arm around *my* shoulder, which was where it should be surgically attached. He steered me inside the building and down the long corridor toward the upper school annex.

"How many times do I have to tell you?" he said as we walked. "I've never cheated on a girlfriend in my life."

"You've never stayed with a girlfriend long enough to cheat on her," I said.

First period on Monday, Wednesday and Friday was Love Stories. I'd get to start the day with Noel three mornings a week. As we approached the classroom door, he maneuvered me into a nook under one of Brownstone's hallway arches (the building was rife with Gothic touches; it was built 150 years ago as a cloister for aspiring nuns). He pressed his body against me and kissed me. Instantly, from only the wee bit of contact, my breathing and pulse quickened.

"Jealousy *is* a charming quirk," I said, my anger melting.

"You don't have to worry," he said. "I'd never cheat on you. If Angelina Jolie walked down this hallway naked and begged me to have sex with her, I wouldn't do it."

"Not in front of all these people," I said. "What if she appeared like a mist in your room and held a gun to your head?"

"In that case, I'd do it," he said. "But I wouldn't enjoy it."

"You'd be thinking of me the whole time," I said.

"Then I would enjoy it."

The bell rang.

Together (languid sigh), in the midst of our own Love Story, we walked into class. Liza and Stanley were seated in the back. We snagged desks by them. I put my backpack on the floor and took out my laptop. I'd only just pushed the START button when Angelina Jolie walked into the classroom.

Not the real Angelina Jolie. A dead ringer for her. Except this woman was blond, with bigger boobs. And younger, too. In her midtwenties at most. She picked up the cursor pen and wrote her name on the digital whiteboard.

"Matilda Rossi," she spoke as she wrote, her voice the sound equivalent of hot chocolate—and not the just-add-boiling-water mix. Her tone was dark, smooth, rich, as if a thousand cocoa beans had liquefied and poured forth from her puffy-lipped mouth.

"Love and passion," she said. "The magic and danger they bring. That's what I'm here to teach. I'm going to take you places. New, mysterious, secret places. And you're going to like it."

I looked at Noel. His jaw, completely unhinged, had dropped to the floor. Stanley Nable's tongue had suddenly grown ten inches and was hanging low enough to wet his shirt. A quick check confirmed that every boy in the class was equally smitten. And every girl, including Liza, was staring at Matilda Rossi like a goddess, a Venus to emulate, or at least get makeup tips from.

But not me. I wasn't wondering what brand of moisturizer she used, or cleaning my desk with drool.

I was praying. Low and soft. "Dear God, please let sweet, dear Ms. Barbaloo have a speedy recovery."

Two

I had no objection, in theory, to Matilda Rossi's impressive physical presence. Any woman had the inalienable right to flaunt her yellow hair and big boobs if she wanted to. I respected that choice. I wouldn't condemn a sister female who opted to strut around like a sorority slut.

However, theory was one thing. Raw, reactive emotion was another. I hated Matilda Rossi on sight because she was beautiful. I wasn't proud of it, but I was grimly accepting of my own limitations as a human being.

Ms. Rossi said, "We'll begin by reading *Romeo and Juliet.* Has anyone read it before?"

A few hands went up, including Noel's. Sorry to report, Noel was a hand raiser. A sharer. A carer. He couldn't wait to offer an opinion or win the gold star for class participation. A few months ago, when we were at odds, I was eye-twitchingly annoyed by his incessant chatter. And now that I loved him? I still hated it.

"Good, good," said the blond teacher, nodding at the raised palms. "*Romeo and Juliet*, as you probably know, is a play. To experience the story the way Shakespeare originally intended, we're going to read it aloud. I've been told Brownstone is packed with acting talent. Has anyone here performed in school plays?"

Again, Noel's hand reached for the ceiling. I groaned, couldn't suppress it. The sound drew Ms. Rossi's attention to the back of the room. Right to Noel's straining outstretched arm.

"The dark-haired young man in the back," said Ms. Rossi. "Yes, you. Would you please stand up? Thanks. My, oh my, you sure are tall!"

Noel said, "You sure are pretty."

No, he didn't say that. But he was thinking it! I could read his mind easily from one desk away.

Ms. Rossi said, "What is your acting experience?"

Noel answered, "I was Gandalf in *The Hobbit* last year."

"Yes, you would make anyone else on stage look short," said Ms. Rossi gratuitously. "You'll be perfect as Romeo."

Noel smiled, blushed (!), practically curtseyed.

Bastard!

"And I," said Ms. Rossi, smiling at Noel, "will play Juliet."

Every boy in the class hooted or whistled. Stanley, sitting next to Liza, reached across two desks to give Noel a knuckle thump.

My heart dropped to my gut. It would have fallen farther, but I was sitting down.

"Yes? In the back? You, with the orange sweater?" said Ms. Rossi.

The eyes of the room turned toward me. I had no clue why I was the sudden focus of attention. And then I realized: I'd raised my arm and was waving it frantically in the air.

Lowering it, grinning sheepishly, I said, "Sorry, my arm slipped."

"Excuse me?"

"It was an accidental hand raise."

"What is your name?"

I groaned (inwardly this time) and said, "Dora Benet."

"If you have something to say to the class, Ms. Benet, you should have the confidence and conviction to do it," said Ms. Rossi.

Liza shot me her wide blue-eyed "What, you worry?" grin.

I said, "I think it'd be a better idea, for the education of the entire class—we're here to learn!—if the part of Juliet were read by a student."

"Are you volunteering yourself?" Ms. Rossi asked.

"I guess, *yes*, I am."

Ms. Rossi said, "Aren't you the little go-getter."

A titter rippled across the rows. Only one way to deflect ridicule. I laughed along, giggling with gusto, sounding like a frightened pony.

Ms. Rossi smiled at the class. On her cheeks, dimples appeared. They were so deep you could plant tomatoes in them. "I've found, Ms. Benet, that if students play both of the romantic leads in this play, the rest of the class tends to project too much into the reading. It's a distraction from the language."

I could see her point. "That's ridiculous!" I blurted.

Ms. Rossi's eyes blazed, burning a hole in my forehead (all the better to pour knowledge into my brain?). "Ms. Benet, I'd like you to read the part of Juliet's fat, homely, elderly widowed nurse. She's the comic relief. That seems to fit you."

"Fit" was an apt word. I was one breath away from throwing one. Then Ms. Rossi said, "Now. Which one of you handsome boys would like to play Mercutio?"

Three

"Don't worry, Dora. You were *fine*," said Liza at Chez Brownstone, the school's cafeteria, catering to the organic, whole-
grain and raw juicing needs of the student body.

Eli asked, "What did she do?"

Noel, Stanley and Eric, our boyfriends, were seated a comfortable distance away at the end of our long table, their heads
together, lascivious grins on their faces.

"I've got a breakthrough diet idea," I said, pushing away
my vegetarian hummus wrap sandwich. "The My Boyfriend's
a Leering Idiot Diet. Makes any self-respecting girl too nause-
ated to eat."

"So you don't want that?" asked Liza, who constantly
struggled to keep her curves from becoming rolls.

I glanced at Noel, his hands cupping the air suggestively.

He could be miming the shape of Ms. Rossi's hips, or a basketball. "Take it," I said, pushing the sandwich at Liza.

Eli said, "Eric is planning a big story on this Matilda Rossi person. He has an appointment to photograph her for the *Brief*. Considering your strong reaction to her, I should probably tag along."

"Keep an eye on him?" Liza asked.

"Eric? Please. Like he'd do anything," said Eli. "I'd just like to take a look at her for myself."

Eli was born in Communist China, abandoned on a hilltop by her teenage mother, discovered by a farmer and left at an orphanage. When she was two years old, she was adopted and brought to America by her parents, Anita and Bertram Stomp, then in their midforties, now as old as my grandparents. Before Eli lost her first tooth, she had already seen enough misery for a lifetime. She was easily annoyed. She had a bit of a temper. But Eli did not ruffle (with one exception, which was my fault, so it won't be recounted here). The possibility that Eric Brainard might swoon over Matilda Rossi was not nearly enough to upset her.

"You're so strong," I observed. "I'm so weak."

"You are truly pathetic," agreed Eli. "It's not like a teacher is a serious threat."

"But the idea Noel would find anyone else attractive," I whined. "He should have eyes only for me."

"His dick is only for you," said Eli. "What do you need his eyes for?"

"I don't want his dick!" I said, way too loudly.

That made Noel, Stanley and Eric look over at us.

"You know you do," said Liza while chewing.

"Jealousy is the most useless emotion," said Eli. "That, or guilt."

"My two biggest hits," I groused. "Is Eric writing a profile of Rossi to go with the picture?"

"I assume," said Eli.

"I wonder if she has a dark past."

"You suspect she's like one of those insane teachers who seduces her adolescent students and then cries about her addiction to Zoloft on *A Current Affair*?" asked Eli.

I shrugged. "Ever notice how all of those perv teachers are blond? Ms. Rossi is blond. Ergo, Ms. Rossi is a perv."

Liza, also of the yellow-haired persuasion, said, "I liked it better when all blondes were stupid."

Stanley Noble slid down the bench toward us. "Ready to go?" he asked. Eric and Noel followed scoot.

Liza said, "Guess what? Dora thinks that—*oofff*!" My elbow in her ribs prevented the slip. Liza had a big mouth. She couldn't help it. She was born without guile.

Stanley asked, "Your house after school?"

Liza's sunshiny demeanor clouded over. She said, "Gary will be there."

"Oh," said Stanley. "My house?"

She said, "I have to look at bridesmaid dresses."

"Anything but pink," said Eli. "Or purple, or baby blue. Or sea foam green."

Liza would be her mom's maid of honor. Eli and I were

to be bridesmaids. I'd never been in a wedding before. And what a wretched way to begin. No one understood why, exactly, Stephanie Greene wanted to marry Gary Glitch. He was the opposite of her first husband, Liza's dad, Ryan, who up and moved to Bermuda three years ago to run snorkel boat tours. I could see that Gary was technically "handsome" in a men's-razor-commercial kind of way (no style *at all*). He made money on Wall Street. But any good qualities were erased by his major bad one.

"Has Gary moved in?" I asked.

Liza was rendered mute by the thought. Finally, Stanley said, "Seems like he's always there."

Eric Brainard, who wasn't as well informed about the tension in Liza's home as the rest of us, said, "I'm sensing a strong dislike. What's wrong with the guy?"

Noel answered for Stanley. "Liza's future stepfather objects to her having a black boyfriend."

"Oh," said Eric.

"Don't say 'stepfather,' " said Liza.

Four

Long first day back. I begged off from after-school social-izing and went home. I climbed the two flights of stairs to our duplex apartment, opened the door, walked through the short hallway to the dining room table, where I dumped my stuff, and then wandered toward the living room. And that was when I saw the horror.

I would describe the sight, but then it would lock into my brain, and honestly, the idea of seeing that again chilled me to the marrow.

On reflex, I spun around and ran into the kitchen. I could hear Mom and Dad rustling on the couch, scrambling to cover themselves.

"Dora! You're home early!" squeaked Mom once she'd arranged herself and found me in the fetal position on the kitchen floor. "Your dad and I are working on the 'Afternoon Delight' chapter in *His-and-Her Romance*, and we thought we'd road-test some of our recommendations."

"Get a room!" I pleaded. "Not the living room. The *bed-room!*"

"You're overreacting," she said, a bit miffed. "And, frankly, it's insulting. All we were doing was—"

"For the love of God, woman, don't say it!"

"Come along, Gloria," said Dad, taking Mom by the hand and pulling her out of the kitchen. "Dora needs to wash out her eyes with soap."

They went up to the second floor of our duplex. I heard the door of their bedroom close and lock. I got up on all fours, dry-heaved a few times, and then felt strong enough to stand.

I would far prefer it if Mom and Dad wrote an advice book called *His-and-Her Celibacy*.

A few minutes later, Joya came in. I was leaning over the sink when I told her what I'd had the misfortune to witness.

She shrugged and said, "I think it's sweet that they have passion for each other after twenty years of marriage."

Joya, an immature girl of just fourteen, understood nothing of the way of the world. "You're mental," I said. "The issue isn't whether Mom and Dad have—and it pains me to say this—*passion* for each other. It's that I had to see it."

"You watch sex scenes in movies all the time."

The girl's denseness had no measure. "You're right," I said. "Watching a couple of paid actors, in two dimensions, on a movie screen, is exactly the same experience as catching my own parents in the act. And don't ask what act. I couldn't possibly say the words. Blisters and sores would immediately form in my mouth."

"Ben and I have been talking," said Joya, speaking of her best (and only) friend (of late, boyfriend).

"I'm glad to hear it, since the two of you spend forty hours a week together."

"I mean, talking about doing things."

Conveniently, I was still leaning over the sink. The idea of my little sister doing anything remotely . . . sexy . . . was just as revolting as Mom and Dad's action sequence.

"That's completely out of the question!" I said. "You're way too young."

Joya shot me the same insulted look Mom just had, on nearly the same face (Joya was Mom's Mini Me). "We're as old as Romeo and Juliet," she replied.

Not those two again. "Yeah, and look at how that turned out. Miserable and dead after three dates."

"Sex can be some grand adventure," she said, "that you go on for free. The experience will add dimension to my art."

"You don't even wear a bra yet."

"I was hoping we could talk," she said. "I have some questions. Like, when we're kissing, I get certain feelings, you know, like glittering blue sparkles up and down my legs, but I was curious about when the feeling turns into a melty, reddish purplish blob that—"

"Enough!" I yelled. "I don't want to hear about your glittery blue sparkles and your purple melty blob. Keep your spar-kles and your blobs to yourself. Please."

Joya's chin quivered. She threw her backpack on the floor, spun out of the kitchen and stomped upstairs to her room. She closed her door, shall we say, *aggressively*.

I had the golden touch with my family today.

With a chilling flash of insight, it occurred to me that Joya was a lot less anxious about physical contact than I was, and she was three years younger. Could be a birth order thing.

But fourteen! If I were in charge, I'd forbid Joya from seeing Ben ever again. I considered going up to my parents' room and telling them that sweet harmless Benjamin Teare, who I'd once thought of as soon-to-be-gay Ben, was actually a (hetero)sexually precocious maniac. Mom and Dad had to know the truth about the boy Joya spent so much time with. I guess the responsibility was on me. I'd have to tell them.

And I would have, too, but when I got to their bedroom door, I heard a loud squeal and a giggle and had to retreat to my room and cover my head with a pillow.

Five

On occasion, when alone in my room, I go into my closet, close the door, turn on the light and study my face in the mirror. Full length, the mirror hung on the door. Sometimes I brought a chair in there so I could sit. Which I did tonight, immediately after an awkward dinner with the fam.

I turned on the light and peered into the glass. I had a decent face. My dad thought I was gorgeous, stunning, a "looker." But since I was the seventeen-year-old female version of him, his opinion was biased. I had light brown hair that some might call tawny. My nose: pert. Skin: clear with a dusting of faint freckles on the bridge of the nose. Zits weren't my bane; I was blessed. I was thin, not skinny. Average height, average weight, average wardrobe. What vaulted me into the above-average category overall were my hazel eyes, which could go from gold to gray, hitting some blues and greens in between.

I'd had bangs—or "fringe," as the English called them—since I was a toddler. They were in an awkward stage at the moment, thanks to a few wrong turns with a stylist last semester. Wisps were re-forming now, and I was relieved. I felt naked without them. My trademark bangs were one of the reasons certain Ruling Class members called me Fringe Girl. The other reason was that I existed on the outskirts, at the edge of Brownstone's social structure. I hovered above the Teeming Masses by only a thread, which could be severed at the whim of Sondra Fortune, queen of the Ruling Class, my sworn enemy.

Sondra and I had traded places and back again last semester. Like cream, Sondra would always rise to the top no matter how far she'd fallen—for instance, in the October social revolution I'd staged and executed. By November we'd returned to our previously held positions, where we both felt more comfortable. I'd suffered mightily for my two weeks at the top. Not her. Sondra coasted down, and coasted right back up. Everything was easy for her, thanks to her family wealth, exotic beauty (half black, half Japanese) and ruthlessness. In the aftermath of our melee, she'd wound up with Vin Transom, my ex. I walked away from our scuffle with Noel.

"What on earth could he possibly see in me?" I asked out loud.

My pores are huge, I thought as I peered into the mirror. Cavelike. Bats could live inside. If you yelled into them, you'd hear an echo.

I'd had enough therapy (forced on me by my parents like gifts—shrink wrapped) to know mirror talks as such weren't good for me. Too much self-criticism could turn me into a nega-holic. Not long ago, I'd tried positive affirmation. Gave myself booster shots. I was my own cheerleader. I had alarming pep.

Lately, though, my inner Simon Cowell had come out of hiding. And he never had anything nice to say.

Chirp. My cell. I flipped open the phone. "Hello."

"Hey," said Noel.

"Hey."

"I couldn't find you after school," he said. "I looked all over."

"I was looking for you. Oh, man!" I said, trying to make it sound sitcomic. You would see the split screen: Noel walking into Chez Brownstone, me walking out a different door. Both of us befuddled. On a sitcom, though, we'd find each other in the end. I hadn't wanted to be found today.

He said, "So what're you doing now?"

"Nothing."

"Want me to come by?"

It was nine o'clock. I said, "It's late."

"Just for a good-night kiss," he offered.

"You'd walk five blocks through the snow just to give me a kiss?"

"For you, Dora, I'd walk six blocks."

I laughed, and a bluish sparkly shimmery melty feeling pulsed under my skin. (Curse Joya.)

"See you in ten," I said.

"I've already got my coat on."

We hung up, and for a glittery few minutes I let myself feel treasured, honored, adored. If I lived to be a thousand, I couldn't imagine a greater joy. Noel was worth all the plasma TVs in the world. He was acceptance into Harvard, Yale and Dartmouth.

Since he was braving the frozen night, he deserved me at my level best. I spritzed and brushed. I rolled on gloss and changed out of track pants and T-shirt, into a black cashmere sweater, jeans and three-year-old Uggs.

"Goingoutforasecondberightback," I shouted as I pranced out of our apartment and down three flights to our two front doors. I flung the first door open and stepped into the unheated space between the doors. Peering out the street window, I rubbed my arms, jogged in place to stay warm and waited for Noel.

And waited. I would have to dry-clean the cashmere from jogging in it so long. I tried to go back through the second door and wait in the heated lobby. But the door was locked. In the flurry of anticipation, I'd let it close behind me instead of propping it open. I considered buzzing my parents to let me in, but then I'd have to do it again after Noel left. I decided to stay where I was and be patient.

So I waited. And waited. Glaciers formed during the time I spent in the vestibule. Continents drifted. Species of frog evolved into lizards. Where the hell *was* he? I wondered, shivering, my gloss icing over on my lips. "Fuck this," I announced finally. Finger poised at the buzzer, I heard the gentle tapping on the outside window.

I saw the shape of a head and a waving mitten. I had to wipe a circle on the inside of the window to clear the glass. As I wiped, Noel emerged, from hair to scarf, his glorious face in between. He was smiling at me. Instantly, my shell of ice cracked.

Opening the outside door, I was hit by a gust of wind and frosty air, and then by the lunging padded body of my boyfriend. He held me against his parka. I pushed him back, unzipped the coat, and then tucked myself into it and against his chest.

"Much, much better," I said into his flannel shirt.

"Sorry I took so long. I had to explain to my mom why I needed to go out so badly," he said, squeezing me.

"What did you tell her?"

"That you had my homework and I had to get it to-night."

"I could have e-mailed it to you."

"Mom doesn't know that."

I took off his glove and pressed his hand against my cheek. Noel's mom, Belinda Kepner, a stay-at-homer, seemed to like me. Sweet, supportive woman, she unnerved me. Not just because she wore an apron and crocheted pillow covers. She was outside my frame of reference. She wasn't anything like my mom, or Anita Stomp, Eli's mother, a lawyer with rows of shark teeth, or Stephanie Greene, an associate something on Wall Street. Working moms were caring mothers, but they had professional interests to think about. Belinda Kepner paid too close attention to her house, her clothes, Noel, the Brownstone "community." It was weird.

I said, "You mean she doesn't read your e-mails and check your Internet history?"

"She wouldn't know how," he said. "She's computer resistant."

"You should make her take a class," I said. "Drag her into cyber-reality."

Noel lifted my chin. "I did not walk five blocks in the cold to talk about my mother."

And then he got what he came for. He kissed me in the dim light of the vestibule, the small space suddenly foggy from the heat of our two bodies, the windows steamed over. I kissed back, straining my neck, Noel's gloved hand lifting me around the waist, his naked hand gripping the back of my neck.

It was some kiss. Definitely worth the wait.

He pulled back, exhaled steam. With urgency, he said, "Come over Wednesday night. My parents have a dinner in the city. We can rehearse *Romeo and Juliet*."

"We have a scene?" I asked, liking the idea of playing the Nurse suddenly.

"A few. You get to call me a scurvy knave," he said.

"Do I have any scenes with Juliet?" I asked. I'd love to call Matilda Rossi a scurvy wench.

"Tons," he said. "I can rehearse those scenes, too." He kissed my neck. "Just come over, okay? Give me a chance, Dora." He kissed my lips. "I swear, you'll be glad you did." His ungloved hand slipped downward, and he felt up the softness of my cashmere.

I said, "Noel, it's not that I don't want to."

He stiffened, his hands leaving me. "So do it, then." He took a step back.

"I can't," I said.

"Why?"

"I have other plans," I lied. "I have to help Liza with some wedding thing."

"Oh," Noel said, zipping his coat. "Too bad."

"Sorry," I said.

"That's okay," he said, resigned. "My parents have a lot of plans coming up—new tax year, new fund-raiser season."

"Great," I squeaked.

Noel zipped up, pulled on his glove, kissed me once, and returned to the frozen night.

I pushed the bell to get back inside. I had to push really hard, a few times, before Mom's voice answered the intercom.

"Can you hear me?" she asked five times, obviously not hearing my response.

The buzzer to unlock the door stuttered, but I managed to get inside. Mom was waiting for me upstairs, arms hanging rigidly at her side (the body language translation of folded arms was "hostile"; Mom hated to give herself away subconsciously).

"What was that?" she asked.

"Noel came by to pick up his homework," I said.

"You could have e-mailed it to him," she said.

"Say, you're right!" I hit myself on the noggin. "I can't believe we didn't think of that. Pretty stupid, huh?"

I played it straight. Mom shook her head at me and said, "Just don't make it a habit."

"What, Noel coming over late?" I asked.

"No," she said. "Being stupid."

Six

"Your line, Nurse," said Ms. Rossi, at the front of the room in a brown wool skirt and a pink blouse. "And try to recite it as if your heart is full of lust. Remember, you're a fat, childless, widowed old hag, and it's your job and duty to attend to the every whim and need of the young and beautiful Juliet. Now, Juliet's mother wants her to marry Paris. And you, Nurse, think Paris is the sexiest man in Verona."

I recited, " 'A man, young lady. Lady, such a man as all the world.' " So far today, I'd already had to read lines with the words "maidenhead," "nipple," "wormwood" and "teat."

I'd decided that acting was not in my professional future. I did like some of the old language, though. Shakespeare used the word "marry" for "indeed."

Ms. Rossi clicked down the row of desks until she was standing between mine and Noel's. By facing me, she gave my beloved an eye-to-cheek view of her rumpy pumpy hump.

"Nurse, is that the best you can do?" she tsked at me. "You're supposed to sound like you've driven into a paroxysm of desire. Your next line is: 'Why, he's a man of wax.' That was how people said 'model gorgeous' in the sixteenth century."

Fascinating. I said, " 'Why, he's a man of wax! He's a flower! A very flower,' " with spasmodic enthusiasm.

"If that's your best, we'll just have to live with it." Ms. Rossi turned around and walked back to the front of the room.

Noel leaned toward me. "Am I a man of wax?" he asked, waggling his eyebrows.

I said, "She hates me."

"Paranoid," he said.

Week I, Scene II
The Brief basement office, Wednesday afternoon

"She looks fat," said Eli as we looked at the cover of tomorrow's edition of the *Brownstone Brief*. "A blond heifer."

Eric Brainard said, "Fat? No way! She looks like a supermodel. Ms. Rossi sets off the sprinkler system. She's a flesh-and-blood fire drill. She . . . Okay, I'll stop."

Eli was giving him one of her scary, inscrutable stares that could mean she was (1) wondering what to have for dinner or (2) imagining the surgical removal of your tongue.

"The only place Matilda Rossi would look fat is at an Anorexics Anonymous meeting," I said. The cover photo was a stunner. I opened the paper and found the two-page profile by Eric. "Tell me she's a wanted fugitive," I said to him.

Eric laughed. "She's wanted, all right."

"She claims to be a law-abiding citizen," said Eli.

"Like we should believe that," I said.

Eric said, "You girls strive to be beautiful and intelligent, but when you see a living breathing example of a woman who has achieved your goals, you instantly distrust her."

"Your point?" I asked.

"It's possible, even likely, that Ms. Rossi is exactly what she says she is—a twenty-six-year-old woman with a master's in English lit from the University of Massachusetts and three years' teaching experience at a boarding school in New Hampshire."

"Did you call this boarding school?" I asked.

"No," said Eric, "I didn't, Dora, but I'm sure Ms. Ratzenberger did or she wouldn't have hired Ms. Rossi. Matty, I mean. She asked me to call her Matty."

"If you call her Matty," said Eli, "you can call me Never."

Ms. Ratzenberger was the director of the upper school, an ancient administrator who'd hired probably scores of substitutes in her thirty years at Brownstone. I wondered how thoroughly she checked their credentials. I said, "I wouldn't be too sure."

"Why can't you take her at face value?" asked Eric, holding up the newspaper cover story. "And, believe me, this face has value."

Week I, Scene III
Grind, Wednesday late afternoon

I was after a quick jolt of caffeine and five minutes to myself. What I found when I pushed through the glass doors of Grind: Liza and Stanley furiously not speaking to each other on a rust-colored velour couch.

I would have ignored them, but they had cookies.

Liza said to me, "Take. I'm not hungry." Now I knew it was serious.

Stanley said, "Then why'd you make me buy them?" A broad, tall guy, Stanley could win a pout-off against a four-year-old. I sat down next to him, making him the meat of our girl sandwich.

I said to them, "You're fighting." They nodded. "Is it about me?"

"No! It's about the wedding," he said. "Liza is threatening to quit as maiden of honor if I can't be an usher."

"She's making a stand," I said.

"Stephanie is going to blame me for ruining her wedding!" he protested. "And I don't want to be an usher."

"But that doesn't matter," whined Liza. "This is bigger than just the insult to you. Mom needs to take three seconds to see what this marriage will do to her family. She's supposed to think about the welfare of her children. But she's 'me, me, me' all the time."

"She should be 'you, you, you,'" I said.

"Exactly."

"She's using me to piss them off," said Stanley to me. Back to Liza: "You've turned me into a pawn. A black one."

I tapped my chin and tried to channel my parents. I mentally scanned the pages of their best seller *His-and-Her Dating*, searching for advice about compromise.

"Ah!" I said, taking another cookie. "I have the solution!"

"What?" asked Liza and Stanley at once.

"You should completely ignore the problem," I said, "and maybe it'll go away."

Liza groaned, but she smiled, too. She took the cookie out of my hand and popped it in her mouth.

Week I, Scene IV
Upper school locker hallway, Thursday morning

Rounding the corner, first thing in the morning, before I'd had coffee, I had the misfortune of bumping into Sondra Fortune. She was with her evil twin henchgirls, Lori and Micha Dropov. They were huddled together next to Sondra's locker.

"Fringe Girl," barked Sondra, "get over here."

Slavishly, I complied. "How can I be of service?" I asked, trying to sound ironic.

"Something has to be done," said Sondra, "about your

substitute English teacher. Matilda Rossi." She held up a copy of the *Brief*. The photo covered the entire front page, like a centerfold. Above the fold showed Ms. Rossi from the waist up. Below the fold, Ms. Rossi from the waist down, in a strikingly short skirt. No shorter than the ones we all wore last spring. But on a teacher in her mid-twenties, it just seemed wrong.

"You'd think there was an age limit on ruffles," I said.

"You're friends with Eric Brainard," said Lori Dropov, sneering at me from behind five layers of red lipstick. "Can't you *do* something about this?"

"About what, exactly?" I asked. "He ran the story in the paper and, by tomorrow, birdcage liner."

"Follow me," said Sondra.

"Don't I always?" I asked.

She led me around the corner and into Chez Brownstone. Lori and Micha followed. I huffed to keep up with the clip of their scissor-thin legs. I figured the Ruling Classers would veer to the left into the food service area, where we'd purchase coffee and discuss the myriad ways I could make Sondra's life easier, but Sondra surprised me by bearing right. She stopped at the first step of the stairway on the east wall of the cafeteria.

I gulped. At the top of the steps there was a room. Only teachers, staffers and administrators had access. It was called the teachers' lounge, aka the Forbidden Zone. It was where teachers performed satanic rituals on students who didn't make healthy snack choices. All kids were unilaterally banned from the Zone, upon punishment of death, unless they were reporting a fire, earthquake or terrorist attack. And even then, intruders would get detention.

"Notice anything different?" asked Sondra.

That morning, the usually dusty and deserted Stairway to Hell was crowded. With minions? I said, "Boys." Dozens of them, lower to upper schoolers. Each held a copy of the *Brief* and wore an impish smile.

"Let's go," said Sondra as she steamrolled through the throng, throwing her pointy elbows, shoving an eighth grader with such force that he nearly flew over the railing into the condiments table below. The Dropovs and I followed in her wake.

At the top of the stairs, the frosted glass door was held open. The line of boys continued into a cavernous, windowless lounge. The eerie, dark space was crammed with old couches and armchairs, the kind you'd find in a haunted library. Bookshelves lined the walls. On every flat surface—lathe-legged tables and the soapstone mantel—along with a lining of dust, sat gilded candleholders and pictures in silver frames.

Zoinks, I thought. The room was totally creepy. I imagined the empty chairs filled with now long-dead nuns from a hundred years ago, in black habits and bird-winged wimples, sipping tea in chattering cups.

In the back of the room, at the head of the line of boys, Matilda Rossi sat behind a huge ornate oak desk. She held a Sharpie in her hand.

She's signing autographs, I thought to myself.

Sondra, standing at my side, clicked her tongue with disgust. "Ms. Ratzenberger gave her the use of the Zone until they can get the funky smell out of Ms. Barbaloo's office."

"What smell? Old lady?" I scanned the line of boys, looking for (too) familiar faces.

Lori's button nose wrinkled. "Her wastebasket wasn't emptied before the winter break."

"What was in it?" I asked.

"Sushi," said Micha. "Salmon skin."

"Is that—it is. Look, Sondra. It's Vin," I said, catching the eye of my ex.

When he saw us, he tried to hide behind his tracklete friends. I was pretty sure Lori had spotted him before I did. I did her the favor of outing him so she didn't have to. Sondra was definitely a kill-the-messenger type.

Upon hearing his name, Sondra spun around—hair flying, grace of a swan (she really was gorgeous)—and located her crouching boyfriend.

Busted, he stood upright, quite impressively. He didn't shrivel like a grape in the sun. Realizing he was caught, he squared off to take his punishment like a man. A man of few words. And one of them was: "Hey."

Sondra answered him with rapidly flaring nostrils and three hair flips in lethal succession. "What, exactly, do you think a substitute teacher's autograph is worth?"

He said, "She used to be a model."

"So was I!" said Sondra. "I don't see you waiting on line for my autograph." (N.B.: Her modeling career began and ended when she was eight and appeared in an ad for Gap Kids.)

Her arms crossed, chin jutting forward, Sondra waited for Vin to respond.

He said, "————." Which was a whole lot of nothing.

Floating unspoken words hung in the air, like a toxic fog. I learned about a new weapon against Sondra that morning. Should I ever need to use it. To make her squirm, give her a silence attack. She lasted no more than ten seconds under the pressure.

Still glaring at Vin, Sondra barked, "Fringe!"

"Present," I replied.

"Noel Kepner is at the front of the line." Without removing her eyes from Vin, Sondra lifted her long, slender arm and pointed all the way down the queue of boys. And there he was. My boyfriend, a copy of the *Brief* in hand.

Noel noticed me, too. He smiled and waved like a wagging golden retriever puppy, innocent, unafraid, tragically, stupidly happy to see me. I burned carpet up to the front of the line, right as Noel was handing his newspaper to Ms. Rossi.

"For posterity," he said politely to her.

She smiled at both of us and said to me, "This is completely embarrassing."

"How true," I said, glaring at Noel.

She scribbled some words on his *Brief*. He thanked her, and then we walked out together. Sondra and the Dropovs were gone. I noticed Vin was still on line. Whatever mind tricks Sondra tried to control him with had failed.

I snatched the paper out of Noel's hand. Ms. Rossi had written, "Dear Noel: I'm glad we'll be seeing so much of each other this semester! [Heart symbol] Matilda Rossi."

"Heart," I said, handing it back.

He shrugged. "Doesn't mean anything."

"It's sickening," I blurted. "Noel, are you aware of the phenomenon of teachers seducing their teenage students? There were three separate incidents in Connecticut a few years ago. I'm bringing this up not because I suspect Ms. Rossi of any wrongdoing. I just worry about your naïveté. You're too trusting, Noel. It frightens me. For your sake."

"Good to know you're looking out for me," he said, folding the paper and slipping it into his shoulder bag.

"There is evil in the world, Noel. You shouldn't assume every pretty woman on the street is some harmless chirpy." I paused. "That said, Ms. Rossi suffers from a pathological need for attention. Insisting on being Juliet. Posing for that photo."

"She posed for the interior shots. Eric didn't shoot the cover," corrected Noel. "It's from an old J.Crew catalog. Eric edited out the canoe. And the Labrador."

He'd left in the boobs. And the legs.

We came to the bottom of the stairs. I checked the clock on the wall. Ten minutes before class. A bell was about to ring.

Seven

"Basic analogy: Black is to white as cold is to hot. They're *opposites*," said Mrs. Strombone, my sixtysomething neighbor. She dressed 1980s style, in blazers with shoulder pads, big chunky faux jewelry and pleated trousers in various shades of tired. "Repeat," she said, tapping a nail on the blackboard.

Eli, Liza and I recited, "Black is to white as cold is to hot," along with the handful of other high school juniors in Mrs. Strombone's ongoing course ("The Heights of College Campaigning"), consisting of SAT prep and, next year, college application assistance. For ten Saturdays, I had to sit in her claustrophobic basement "classroom" and learn analogies, sentence completion, vocabulary and critical reading. Or, as I think of it, FUN! FUN! FUN!

All of the students in the room knew that analogies were

no longer a part of the SATs. Mrs. Strombone, unfortunately, wasn't up to speed. She hadn't changed her curriculum in ten years. Early on in her college campaigning career, Mrs. Strombone had great success, getting two kids into Harvard in one year. Since then, she'd kept her business going by dropping the H-bomb at every opportunity. Parents too busy to review her outdated course work just signed on the dotted line. Mom and Dad had no choice but to send me. Mrs. Strombone lived across the street from us on Garden Place, and she had been reminding Mom since I was twelve years old that college campaigning would give me an "edge." Apparently, an edge was much to be desired. Eli and Liza agreed to take the course with me. Liza was thrilled to get out of her house every Saturday. Eli was taking another course in Manhattan, but didn't want to be left out. Since we'd all rather take naps with our eyes open than correct Mrs. Strombone's analogies gaffe, we said nothing.

Liza leaned over to me and whispered, "I don't care about college. I want to move to Bermuda and teach snorkeling."

"Follow in your dad's flipper steps?" asked Eli.

"Basic analogy," I whispered. "Matilda Rossi is to cradle robber as Paris Hilton is to shameless bimbo."

"I think you're getting the hang of it," said Eli, who'd gotten a perfect score on her PSATs. She was a National Merit Scholar, too. I'd done okay. I could have done better, but I rebelled against the process and dithered. Why should a test taken at age sixteen be so important? Why should the rest of your life be dependent on a score?

I looked over at Eli, impressed by her shiny black hair, dry-cleaned sweater set, notebook page neatly marked, pen full of ink. She was a lock on whatever college she wanted. Piano prodigy, on track for valedictorian, a colorful past as an abandoned Chinese baby. Since she'd started dating Eric Brainard (himself born with the Ivy League stamp of approval on his forehead), Eli had been writing tart editorials for the *Brief*. She had beauty, brains, talent, ambition. The only option unavailable for Eli was professional athlete.

Liza, meanwhile, had been spending the seminar hour thus far doodling bunnies, kitties and floating eyes in her notebook. Her pen had a well-gnawed end, which was, at present, resting on her bottom row of teeth.

My notebook was clean of both doodles and analogies. I'd lost the hour of valuable edge-acquiring time watching everyone else, struggling not to worry about my future. My grades were decent, but not stellar. My scores were unexceptional. I had no God-given talents like Eli, nor was I willfully oblivious to what their absence meant for my future prospects, like Liza.

Tapping again on the blackboard, Mrs. Strombone said, "A college campaign is to your future as blank is to blank. Anyone want to try it? How about you, Dora?"

"Okay," I said. "A college campaign is to my future as a bicycle is to a fish."

Eli whispered, "I know you're getting the hang of it."

Mrs. Strombone was not amused. She was sure to tell my mother I'd been disrespectful. I'd pay for it later. The price of an acid wit. Since I'd resolved to live in the moment (as of a few moments ago), I soaked in the muffled titters of the other students. Even those three saintly boys from St. Andrews (the other, snootier Brooklyn Heights private school) were grinning.

Mrs. Strombone said, "I can see that we've reached a point of diminishing returns. That's all for today."

"Grind?" asked Eli as Mrs. Strombone passed around packets of homework.

Liza said, "I can't."

"Let me guess—wedding invitations?" I asked. Of late, Liza had been chained to a chair and forced to apply her adequate calligraphy skills to envelopes.

"We're picking up Matt at the airport," she replied.

Matt was Liza's older brother, a junior at Northwestern in Evanston, Illinois. I remembered him as an obnoxious juvenile fuzzy-chinned pest who used to spy on us when we'd lived in the same building on Hicks Street.

"Would you consider Matt officially estranged, or merely alienated?" I asked.

"Alienated," said Liza. "It's not that there's tension between Mom and him. It's just that they have so little in common. He hasn't met Gary yet."

"Should be a train wreck." That was Eli.

Liza smiled and shrugged. "A girl can hope."

We waved good-bye to Liza outside of Mrs. Strombone's, and then Eli and I walked across the street to my building. Since Mom and Dad were away for the night (researching the his-and-her romanticness of a fancy Manhattan hotel), I felt safe about bringing Eli home. Mom had a tendency to bad-ger my friends for information, a practice I called emotional archaeology. She insisted she did it out of caring and genuine interest in Liza's and Eli's lives. And that was true, to a point. I knew that underneath all her caring and interest, Mom seized any opportunity to spew her wisdom. She didn't smoke. She rarely drank. She didn't use recreational drugs (to my knowl-edge). But she was seriously addicted to giving advice. There was no stopping her. Unless, of course, she had nothing to comment on.

Eli and I climbed the flights to our duplex. I put my key in the lock.

Eli said, "Where's Romeo today?"

I said grumpily, "How should I know? I don't have a leash on him. I'm not his warden. Noel is free to move about the city."

"He hasn't called," Eli guessed, correctly.

I twisted the knob and pushed the door open. We walked down the short hallway, powder room on the right, coat clos-et on the left. We emerged into the spacious dining room, kitchen to the right. Out of the corner of my eye, to the left, I noticed movement on the living room couch.

My first thought: Burglar! Two of them!

My second thought: Mom and Dad, at it again.

But it wasn't my parents. The couple disentangled them-selves in a flash. Joya shrieked like a harpy. Ben Teare cursed in a decidedly not-gay way.

It was even worse than walking in on Mom and Dad. At

least Ben and Joya were fully dressed, which, despite my shock and revulsion, flooded me with relief.

Eli just stood there, grinning like she'd discovered gold.

Joya said, "A little privacy!"

Eli said, "If you wanted privacy, you should be upstairs."

"Don't give her ideas!" I shouted.

"It's hardly an idea," said Eli. "Anyone with two brain cells to rub together would have thought to go into a room with a door."

Ben, whom I'd known since he was five, stood up suddenly, blushed scarlet and sat back down. A pillow pressed to his lap, he blurted, "You're supposed to be at some SAT class."

"You conniving little hedonists," I said. "Ben, get out."

Joya, the most even-tempered, peaceful person I knew—until now—spat violently. "You can't tell him what to do."

"The hell I can't. Let's go, Ben. Now. This way." I rooted in the closet for his coat. "Don't forget this. Cold out there."

Ben, sensing the fun was over, limped toward me to get his coat. He put it on, grudgingly, and said to Joya, "I'll call you later." I held the door open, then slammed it behind him.

Joya was already blubbering about her humiliation. Eli sat beside her on the couch and tried to comfort her. They'd known each other since Joya was a newborn. Eli, an only child, had taken Joya as a surrogate little sister.

"There, there, Joya," she said. "Dora's in a mood today."

"This isn't about me!" I raved. "I don't like coming home every day and finding people fooling around on the couch. This is not wholesome family behavior!"

Eli said, "I had no idea you were such a prude."

"It's a clean job, but someone's got to do it," I said.

"You're just jealous!" said Joya, her eyes wet and shining.

I groaned. I'd made the mistake of being honest with her about my jealousies a couple of months ago. About her effortless beauty, her inner peace, how she seemed to float through life. I looked at her now, grim and flushed on the couch, and saw with a sudden wallop that Joya had changed. Sometime over the last month or two, when I wasn't looking, she'd shed her airy-fairy wings. The babyish glittery pixie dust glow was nearly gone. Joya had crossed into adolescence.

I said, "When Mom and Dad aren't here, I'm in charge. I have to be the rational, reasonable, conscientious adult. I'm the responsible party. And it is my opinion that you and Ben are too young for what you were doing. You simply don't have the emotional maturity to handle it. Physical closeness is huge, Joya. Way bigger than you."

Joya glared at me. "Who are you trying to convince?" she asked. "Me, or yourself?"

Eli laughed (!). "She nailed you there, Dora."

I told my dear friend, "Shut the hell up!"

A knock on the door. I flung it open, to find Ben Teare cringing, bundled in his coat, on the other side.

I said, "What?"

He cowered and said, "I forgot my gloves."

Eight

"What do you think is more romantic," asked Mom when she and Dad returned from their field trip, "a walk over the Brooklyn Bridge at night or a candlelit dinner at a restaurant?"

"Walk over the bridge," said Dad.

"Candlelit dinner," said Joya, her eyes flickering like candles, probably thinking of Ben.

"Dora?" asked Mom.

"I'd rather not say."

"Isn't Noel coming over?" asked Mom.

He usually picked me up around sevenish on Saturday nights. It'd been a standing date. But since I hadn't heard from him—no calls, IMs, text messages—I had to assume he was sitting this Saturday out.

I said, "He's busy."

"So it's a family fun night at the Benets?" asked Dad, way too enthusiastically. "Let's play Hearts."

Joya said, "Dad, we're not babies anymore."

Mom and Dad laughed at her tone. It was condescending and rude, and I felt her indignation. My sympathies didn't keep me from laughing at her, too, however. Neither one of us had said anything to our parents about the middle school rumpus I'd interrupted on the couch earlier. So I had something on her.

I said, "I'd love to play Hearts."

Mom said, "You *would*?"

"Do you want it in writing?"

"I expected you to go sulk alone in your room."

"I'm quite capable of sulking and playing Hearts at the same time."

Ring. Landline. Noel called the home phone sometimes. I grinned, relieved to hear from him.

Mom answered. "Hello?"

Her face fell. Like a piano out a window. Dad sensed the sudden change in the room's atmosphere and looked at his wife.

He asked, "Who is it?"

"He's right here," she said. "Ed, it's Patricia O'Hearn."

Dad's eyes bugged. "Patty? You're kidding."

"I wouldn't dare joke about her," said Mom, shoving the phone into his hand.

Dad said, "Maybe I'll take this in the office."

Mom said, "Go ahead, if you want to sleep on the couch."

Joya and I blinked at each other. I'd never heard of this Patty O'Hearn before. *A mystery woman from their past!* How exciting. As far as I knew, Mom and Dad had met in college, dated for a year, got married, had kids, and wrote best-selling advice books together and tra-la-la-ed into the horizon, skipping.

Dad cleared his throat. He said, "Hello, Patty." His eyes glued to the saltshaker, he tried to keep a stone face while he listened. Mom watched, her arms hanging (not folded, never folded) but stiff as steel rods.

"Thank you," said Dad. "We've been very lucky. Yes, that was Gloria who answered. Yup. For almost twenty years."

He dared to glance at Mom. She scowled. He went back to his scrutiny of the salt.

"You're in New York," he said. "SoHo is very close to us. No, no. Brooklyn isn't Outer Mongolia." He laughed. "I'll have to check my schedule. I'm sure Gloria would love to see you, too."

Mom shook her head furiously. She held up her hands in the universally recognized "stop" signal.

He said, "Okay, that sounds good. Sure. I'll tell her. Great to hear your voice, too. Bye." Dad hung up, then placed the phone carefully on the table. He smiled at it, a creeping, fleeting flash of teeth, quickly extinguished.

"So, where were we?" he asked the silent room. "We're playing Hearts. And let's have some ice cream, too."

"Ed, I have some thoughts about the chapter we were working on today," said Mom. "I need to explain them to you. In the office."

Dad sighed. "I was afraid you might."

Mom said, "Girls. Clean the kitchen, please."

Joya and I glanced into the already spotless kitchen. Mom and Dad left the dining room and went into their office, a little room just off the living room. It was about thirty feet from where we sat.

"They're fighting in there, right?" Joya asked. "The really horrible low-talking kind of fight that's worse than yelling."

She seemed genuinely upset, but she was easily disturbed. "I'm thinking ex-girlfriend," I said. "Maybe Dad was with her before he met Mom. Or someone he met *after* he and Mom hooked up." I strained to listen to their hushed, frantic conversation. "Patricia O'Hearn," I said, shaking my head. "Definitely *not* Jewish."

Joya said, "We're all just entertainment for you, aren't we?"

I shushed her so I could listen. Frustrated by their maddeningly low voices, I went up to my room and checked for messages.

Zilch.

Nine

I didn't sleep much. I got up to check for messages every few hours. The loss of beauty sleep took its toll. Perhaps it was best that Noel was avoiding me. Around noon, hunger forced me out of my room and downstairs into the kitchen.

Weirdly, the apartment was empty. On Sundays, usually, Mom and Dad were splayed all over the couch in his-and-her bathrobes, the *New York Times* divided by section (he took Automobiles, Sports, Travel and the Week in Review; she took Arts and Leisure, Styles, Metro, the magazine, and the Book Review), and their ever-present mugs of coffee on the living room table. Joya, like a happy, scrappy puppy, usually sat on the carpet, drawing a new comic book about demon babysitters or unicorn vampires. But instead of that Brooklyn family portrait, I found three notes on the dining room table. I read them in the following order.

Dear Girls:

I'm at the gym. It's been way, way too long since I had a good, heart-pounding torture session with the treadmill. I thought I'd take a sauna and a massage, so don't expect me back soon.

Love,
Dad

Dora and Joya:

Forgive me for not being here to make you breakfast. But then again, even if I were home to serve you, you wouldn't appreciate it. I'm not in the mood to be taken advantage of this morning, or taken for granted, or disrespected. Believe me, for each thing I do that you notice, there are twenty that you don't. I have no idea what your father has planned for dinner this evening. I've already arranged to meet some friends in the city for a late lunch. So. You'll have to make yourselves dinner, too. And I'm not going to feel guilty about it.

Love,
Mom

Joya's note, the one I picked up last, was a drawing of four people, each standing on one corner of a square. Three of the characters (clearly representing Mom, Dad and me) had their backs to each other. One character (Joya and her pixie cut) was facing in.

I put down the sketch. Even though it was rudimentary

(the people were barely more than stick figures), Joya's cartoon stabbed me in the tender spot. Mom's martyr-me note was barely legible. She'd written it faster than she could have ranted it. Since Dad did ninety percent of the cooking, and Joya and I did the cleaning up, meal preparation was a bizarre chore for her to complain about. And Dad writing about going to the gym? He used to jog, like ten years ago. What brought on the exercise jones? Patty O'Hearn?

So who would win Mom's and Dad's contest to see who could avoid the other longer? Honestly, they were behaving with as much maturity as Noel and me. Assuming, as I had, he wasn't calling on purpose.

If only he would. I'd invite him over for some alone-together time. I willed him to call. To come over and fill up this empty, lonely apartment.

Ring. I smiled, remembering that my love with Noel transcended time and space. I could think of him and he'd know. He was right there with me, on the astral plane.

I picked up the kitchen phone and said, "Well, hello there."

Liza said, "Hello, yourself."

Hiding my disappointment, I said, "You're not Noel."

"I need rescuing."

"That bad?"

"Come over and say you have to steal me. That it's an educational crisis."

"The levees broke on *Sesame Street*?"

"Oh, that's *good*," she said. "Tell them we're off on a charitable mission. Some Katrina thing."

"I just got up," I protested. "And it's *cold* out there."

"Dora, this is an emergency," pleaded Liza.

"Give me an hour."

She hung up. I toasted and schmeared a bagel. After eating, I threw on my jeans, a turtleneck, my Uggs (uggly, but *so* comfortable), my Michelin Man down jacket, a pom-pom scarf, a sherpa hat and angora mittens. I braced myself and went outside.

The walk to Liza's in Cobble Hill took fifteen minutes. Leaning hard on the buzzer, my fingers stiff inside my mittens, I was fourteen minutes past frozen. It seemed like forever until someone came to the door.

And as it opened, a light shone from the crack, an ever-widening beam of brilliance until it was broad enough to hit me. From inside my cocoon of winter wrapping I shielded my eyes, squinting into the radiance.

Brief digression: Back in fifth grade, we'd studied the Greek gods of Mount Olympus. In our textbooks, there was a painting of each deity surrounded by his or her props. Hermes had winged sandals. Zeus had a thunderbolt. Dionysus with a jug of wine. Aphrodite on a clamshell, rising from the ocean. Poseidon and his seahorse-drawn chariot. I liked them all, but one god became a fixation, an object of my eleven-year-old lust. Apollo was the god of music, philosophy, wisdom and poetry. He carried a little harp called a lyre and strummed it for the delight of immortals and mortals alike. Apollo was the sun god. His golden hair and blue eyes shone; his skin was bronzed and glowing. I hadn't thought of Apollo or that painting in years. But now, the living, breathing doppelgänger of the sun god was holding open the door to Liza's apartment, smiling down at me.

I stared. My mouth hung open. I may have drooled on my pom-poms.

He said, "Adora Benet! I'd recognize you anywhere, even under that hat." He reached out, put a sun-dipped hand on my shoulder and pulled me inside Stephanie Greene's floor-thru two-bedroom on Pacific Street.

Through five layers of clothing, including the overstuffed down coat, I felt the warmth of his hand.

"Liza's waiting for you in her room," he said casually, as if everything were normal, and I hadn't just been struck dumb.

I said, "Hummina, hummina." Honestly, it was all I could manage.

He laughed (brightly, boisterously) and said, "You're frozen solid. Let me help you out of those clothes."

And then he took me by the mitten. My skin inside the angora ignited. He removed my mittens one by one, rubbing each hand as he exposed my skin to the radiator air. Then unwound my scarf, pulled off my hat, unzipped my coat, and pulled it off my shoulders and down my arms, which he then rubbed briskly.

As he undressed me, I could barely breathe. My cheeks were burning red.

He kept going, lifting my sweater at the hem, and started to pull it over my head. If he'd unbuttoned my jeans and yanked them down to the ankles, I might not have had the willpower to stop him.

Mustering my inner strength (and modesty), I removed his hands from my sweater and pulled it back down. "Matt Greene," I said to the scrawny, obnoxious geek who'd transformed into a tall golden god in Illinois (who'd have believed it?). "What exactly are they feeding you at Northwestern? And how can I get some?"

He laughed. "It has been a while since I've seen you."

"So you're used to you," I said. "I'll need a few minutes to adjust."

"Take your time," he said. "I'll need a few minutes to take you in, too." He openly, one might say *rudely*, appraised my seventeen-year-old self. A fireball careened down my spine. I actually started to sweat. Fifteen degrees outside, and I was burning.

And then Liza thundered down the hallway from her bedroom. "Dora! You're here. Let's go. Now, please, before they make me address another envelope."

"You're not leaving already," said Matt.

"We're not leaving already," I said.

"But our charitable mission awaits," insisted Liza. "Here's your scarf. Here's your coat. Come on."

Stephanie Greene called from the eat-in kitchen at the end of the apartment's long central hallway, "Who was at the door?" The bride-to-be emerged into the corridor and came toward me. She said, "Dora! I'm so glad to see you. Gary! Dora Benet is here."

At the mention of the future stepfather's name, Liza hissed and Matt frowned. He'd already formed an opinion of Gary Glitch, and it wasn't a good one.

Gary poked his head out of the kitchen. He waved limply at me. Gary and I had exchanged no more than ten words in the six months Stephanie had been dating him. For the first three months, Liza had kept her mother's new boyfriend a secret from Eli and me. Or, rather, it wasn't that she kept him from us. She didn't find him newsworthy at first, assuming her mom would dump him in short order and then shower for five hours to wash away the slime. But that hadn't happened. And now they were engaged, for reasons no one could quite figure out, except that Stephanie said he made her feel "secure" and "appreciated."

Secure and appreciated. If that was the most I could hope for in my future marriage, I'd rather be single forever.

I gave Gary the thumbs-up and a toothy (ironic) grin, which made Liza laugh. Gary seemed confused and ducked back into the kitchen, disappearing himself like he'd never really been there.

The Greenes and I stood by the door, smiling awkwardly. Stephanie put an arm around each of her children and said, "It's so nice having the family together. That includes you, Dora."

"Too bad Dad isn't here," said Liza.

Stephanie blanched, and then looked sad. "I'll get back to the invitations. Liza, whenever you're ready to write the name cards."

"Dora and I have a thing. A charitable thing. For Katrina victims," said Liza.

"Oh? A fund-raiser?"

"Sure is," said Liza, putting on her coat. "It's at Brownstone. Nothing major. Just a preliminary meeting. For members of the committee. The fund-raising committee. For the charity. Event."

Liza should have just looked grave and chanted "Katrina." If I'd been Stephanie, I wouldn't have believed a word out of her daughter's mouth.

Matt wanted an out, too. "I'd love to go to Brownstone. Especially on a Sunday."

"Come with!" I bleated. Liza shot me a confused look.

Stephanie pursed her lips and said to her son, "I thought you and Gary could spend some time together. Go to a movie, or to lunch, or play some video games."

"Mom, I'm twenty years old," said Matt, which made my heart flutter.

"Please, Matt," she begged. "For me."

Liza nudged me with her elbow. She mouthed, "Me, me, me."

"It's enough that you want to marry the guy," said Matt. "You shouldn't need me to want you to marry him, too."

"You're right," said Stephanie, her eyes pooling. She had a hair-trigger tear reflex. When she and Ryan had decided to divorce, the waterworks were on full blast for months. "Maybe it's too much to ask that my children want me to be happy." She sniveled. "Gary and I will be perfectly fine here without either of you."

As much as I wanted Matt to come with us, he'd be a bit of a shit to leave his mother like this. He said, "Okay, okay, I'll stay."

Stephanie insisted. "No, leave. I don't want you here if you don't really want to stay."

"I said I'd stay."

"But do you *want* to?" asked Stephanie.

Matt paused and then yelled down the hall, "Hey, Gary!"

From the kitchen, the bridegroom replied, "Yes?"

Matt smiled at his mom and shouted, "How about we have dinner together? Just you and me?"

"No can do," replied Gary. "I've got to head back to the city tonight."

"How about breakfast?" asked Matt.

"I'll be at the office," said Gary.

"Dinner tomorrow night?"

Gary said, "Would love to, but I've got plans."

"Lunch?" asked Matt.

"I'll be swamped at work," said Gary.

Stephanie listened to their exchange, her mouth flat and thin. Matt kissed her on the forehead and said, "I'm going out with the girls now. Okay?"

Stephanie nodded. We quickly suited up and blew out of there. As soon as we hit the stoop, Matt said, "Air. I can breathe again."

Liza said to her brother, "There isn't any fund-raiser meeting or committee."

He laughed. "No shit, Liza."

"Grind?" she asked.

"Isn't there anything closer?" I asked, shivering,

So we went to Smith Street in Boerum Hill. The avenue

(not a street per se) had once been lined with abandoned buildings and decrepit bodegas. Thanks to Brooklyn's burgeoning restaurant scene, it had undergone a transformation from "depressed and crime-ridden" Smith Street to "fabulous and hot" Smith Street in only a few years. Matt left Brooklyn for college at the beginning of the renaissance. He was impressed by the change. "I should come back to Brooklyn more often," he said, looking at me.

We went into Bar Tabac, where we neither drank alcohol nor smoked. We sat at a cozy farm table in the back on a mahogany bench seat, under amber glass windows, against redbrick walls. Our table had a votive that flickered and danced, a single flame that cast a glow and warmed me inside and out. Sitting next to Matt didn't hurt, either.

We ordered cappuccinos and *pommes frites*. Matt told us stories about college, the parties and late nights, people he'd met from all over the country. New York was a melting pot, and you could rub shoulders with citizens of the world on every city block. But Californians were exotic to Brooklynites. Matt lived in a dorm with four of them. While we talked and laughed, I felt sophisticated, wise and witty. This was a far cry from the high drama one always found at our usual Smith Street hangout, Juicy Bar, a protein-shake joint up the block that catered to the pre-alcohol private school crowd.

"So, Dora," said Matt, his knee bumping into mine when he turned to face me, "are you seeing anyone?"

"Yeah, I guess so," I said.

"*Excuse* me?" asked Liza. "She's madly in love with Noel Kepner, and he's totally into her."

"Is that why he hasn't called me in two days?"

"Noel Kepner? I remember that kid," said Matt.

"He's best friends with Stanley," said Liza.

"Two best friends dating two best friends," said Matt. "That's precious!"

"Shut up," I said, swatting him. "It probably won't last anyway. Noel has the romantic attention span of a gnat, and he's apparently forgotten about me already."

"Don't say that," said Liza, offended that I'd be cavalier about Noel.

I shrugged. "It's been tense lately. I haven't told you everything."

"Then tell me," she said.

"Yes, Dora. Do," added Matt, his shining face lit upon me.

I couldn't tell the whole story and confess to Matt Greene that I was terrified of spending alone-together time with Noel. That my stalling could last only so long before I'd have to explain myself, at which point Noel would realize exactly what kind of girl I really was. The chickenshit kind. The girl who hadn't emerged from puberty with the innate sexual expertise of a porn star. I had no clue what I was doing, what he'd be doing, what it all meant and how it'd feel, body, mind and soul. I was amazed that some girls dove blindly into this ocean, bumbling and stumbling along until they were in deep.

But my ignorance wasn't what truly terrified me. I remembered a conversation I'd had with Mom years ago, when we were introduced to health classes at Brownstone about periods and reproduction. I came home and asked her about some finer points. She explained the details, and added, "Dora, you never have to do anything with a boy you don't want to do."

"I *know* that, Mom. You've been telling me since second grade," I said.

"Well, you don't," she repeated.

"But what if I *do* want to do it?" I asked.

Mom didn't have an answer for me then. She probably wouldn't have one now. If the advice maven was stumped, how on earth could I build a bridge over the deepening chasm between wanting and fearing? I marveled at Eli, who'd had sex with two different boys already, seemingly without freaking. But Eli didn't seem to have daily (hourly) wrestling matches with her insecurity. She was a girl of action. Liza's sexual history was shrouded in a cloud of guilt and anxiety. She had impulsively slept with someone last summer for the wrong reasons (to lure the guy back into a relationship), and that mistake had cost her dearly. I wasn't sure what Liza and Stanley did. She was the rare girl who kept her private life private.

"Noel and I seem to have conflicting outlooks," I said. "Let me put it in the form of an analogy. Noel is to the mountaintop as I am to the ski lodge."

Matt laughed. "Here's another one. Dora Benet is to adorable as a *pomme frite*"—he lifted a crisp one and popped it into his mouth—"is to potato."

"Thanks," I said, "for comparing me to a potato."

We smiled at each other. Matt ate another fry. I glanced

across the table at Liza. She frowned and shook her head with one sharp jerk.

When I got home hours later, Dad was locked in the office. Joya was locked in her room. Mom, whom I might have had an emotionally archaeological talk with, wasn't back yet.

Noel had not texted, IMed or called.

Ten

I hovered by Noel's locker for ten excruciating minutes before class on Monday morning. I checked and rechecked my locker contents, trying to look busy and casual. I'd wanted to confront him before class, to clear the air. But that wasn't going to happen. Therefore, the air in English lit was thick and dirty when I walked in. Noel was seated conspicuously far away from my usual desk.

He was on the other side of Stanley. They were laughing about something. It seemed forced. I could play that game, too.

Liza walked in behind me. She looked at Noel and Stanley and said, "They look jolly."

Which made me howl. I laughed and laughed. I busted a gut. It spilled all over the classroom. A few kids looked at me as I guffawed, including Noel.

"Why don't you tell us what is so hilarious, Ms. Benet." The voice came from the front of the room.

I scurried into my chair. "Nothing," I squeaked.

"Couldn't be nothing," said Ms. Rossi, wearing yet another tight skirt and a clinging sweater set. "You were doubled over."

"Uh," I stalled. "Okay. I heard a funny joke."

"Why don't you share it?"

"It's not appropriate for mass consumption."

"Try me," she said.

"Okay." I started, remembering this nugget Dad told me last week. "Here goes. George Bush is in a Cabinet meeting. The secretary of defense says, 'Mr. President, we have reports that Brazilian soldiers were killed in Iraq today.' The president says, 'That's terrible!' and acts very, very upset. The Cabinet members are a bit confused by his reaction. Finally, the president tearfully asks, 'How many is a brazillion?' "

I got a genuine laugh from the class.

Rossi was a tougher audience. "Do you find it funny that soldiers are dying in Iraq?" asked Ms. Rossi.

"No!" I said. "Of course not."

"Do you think you could do a better job of protecting our country than the government?"

I must have shrugged. A few kids laughed. She said, "See me after class, Ms. Benet."

Then she went to the whiteboard and started writing titles: *Romeo and Juliet, Anthony and Cleopatra, Tristan and Isolde, Othello.* I noticed that the boys were watching her ass as she wrote.

She twirled back around and asked, "What do these love stories have in common?"

Noel raised his hand (never missed an opportunity to proclaim). He said, "They're all tragic. The lovers die in the end."

"Correct. Does anyone want to elaborate on why so many love stories have themes of betrayal, pain, suffering, misery, madness and death?"

Noel's arm shot up like a rocket. Ms. Rossi rewarded him with a coquettish smile. She said, "Is Noel Kepner the only student in this class who has courage and intelligence?"

Every boy in the class (save a few who genuinely lacked courage—no one at Brownstone lacked intelligence) flung his arm ceilingward. Every girl in the class lowered her eyes to her desk.

"Ms. Benet," said Ms. Rossi, who would not leave me alone.

"Yes, ma'am," I said.

"Here's your chance to say something useful to the class."

"I'm not qualified to talk about the misery of love," I said nonchalantly.

"Noel?" she asked, tipping her chest in his direction.

He said, "Love stories in literature are tragic because that's often the way love stories are in real life."

And then he stopped talking. Usually, when Noel had the floor, he would sweep every corner of it.

"What do you mean?" she prodded.

Noel said, "Is love a tender thing? It is too rough, too rude, too boisterous, and it pricks like a thorn."

From behind me, someone coughed, "He said 'prick.' " A few people tittered.

Ms. Rossi ignored them, and beamed at Noel. "In case you hadn't realized, class, Noel was quoting Romeo. To which Mercutio responded, 'If love be rough with you, be rough with love. Prick love for pricking, and beat love down.' "

Noel glanced in my direction. I knew then, with a heart-stopping shudder, what I'd suspected all weekend. Noel hadn't been busy. He hadn't been too tired to call. He'd intentionally blown me off to punish me. To prick me (no, not in *that* sense). My mind scrambled to figure out what I'd done to deserve the cold treatment. I couldn't come up with a thing.

I'd been glib with Matt at Bar Tabac, saying that Noel had the relationship attention span of a gnat and that we were too different. Now I wondered if my flirty chatter had truth behind it. Maybe Noel was angry because I wasn't who he wanted me to be. Maybe he'd fallen out of love with me.

Ms. Rossi said, "Let's pick up *Romeo and Juliet* where we left off. Act two, scene one, otherwise known as the balcony scene. The most famous, most quotable scene in English litera-ture. The essence of sexual longing, unfulfilled desire and new love." She gave a deep, breast-heaving sigh and said, "Noel? Shall we begin?"

After school I found Eli in the music room. She was just fin-ishing a private lesson with Mr. Yamora, the music department head, a quiet and intense man who dashed my musical hopes in sixth grade when he flunked me in clarinet. Eli, however, was a piano prodigy and had won the state's high school competition twice. She would have won it last year, too, but she was in the middle of a romantic tug-of-war between Eric Brainard, her current, and Jack Carp, her ex, also a gifted pianist. Eli had been distracted. She'd lost the competition, but she'd learned a valuable lesson.

"I learned you can't be completely trusted!" said Eli now, reminding me of the incident.

"Let's move on, shall we?" I suggested, remembering the guilt.

"Gladly," she said and switched her sheet music. She began playing something full and lovely, with soaring highs and morose lows.

"What's that?" I asked.

" 'Romeo and Juliet,' by Tchaikovsky," she said. "Possibly one of the most famous pieces in classical music. You don't recognize this part? It's in dozens of movies, whenever lovers run toward each other across a flowery meadow in slow motion."

"Yeah, whatever," I said. "Eli, you're a slut. And I mean that in the nicest possible way."

"Go on," she said, tickling the ivories.

"I need to know what's expected of me. And what I should expect."

"Any guy will be overjoyed if you just show up," she said. "And don't expect much from the act. It takes a long time before it stops hurting. And then a lot longer before it feels good."

"Maybe that was the problem with Jack," I said. "You weren't with him long enough."

"Maybe."

"This is how I imagine it with Noel," I said. "We're in my room, the covers pulled up over us. Foreplay, foreplay, foreplay. I get thirsty from all that heavy breathing. I'm trying to stay in the moment and just *feel the feeling,* but my lips are dry and my throat is parched. I say, 'This is heaven on earth, but I need water.' He's torn out of the moment and insulted. The scene devolves from there. It's idiotic, I know. But the logistics. The nonmechanical, or I should say non-anatomical, how-things-work stuff. It confounds me. My fear of sex has been reduced to anxiety about a glass of water."

Eli said, "You are very peculiar, Dora."

"Noel has fallen out of love with me," I said. "So it's useless anxiety."

"Useless anxiety," repeated Eli, playing a lighter melody. "Nice redundancy."

"Easy for you to say," I barked. "You've got the at-one-with-the-cosmos Buddhist genes backing you up. I'm a neurotic Jew. Sex is a troubling subject for my people. Have you read Philip Roth? Ever seen a Woody Allen movie?"

"Imagine how Liza feels," said Eli. "She's Catholic."

We contemplated Liza's handicap. I said, "Lapsed."

"But still," said Eli, "it's in there."

"Have you been over to Liza's lately?" I asked.

Eli laughed. "I've heard all about it, Dora."

"What?" I asked, plinking a piano key. It clanked. Even at random I was tone-deaf.

"You," sang Eli. "Matt Greene. Salivating over each other at Bar Tabac."

"I was just being friendly."

Eli said, "I can't say I blame you. For being *friendly*. I ran into him on the walk to school. He sure has changed."

I sighed, remembering Matt's beauty. And then Eli ruined it. "So," she said. "You were saying how Noel Kepner has fallen out of love with you?"

The music room door opened. Jack Carp, Eli's ex, dressed head to toe in black, including his Chuck Taylors and a vintage Ramones T-shirt, slumped into the room. Seeing Eli, his face brightened, and then collapsed, in the span of one nanosecond. It was sad to behold. The poor guy continued to pine for her. It'd been three months since he'd won the state competition, performing a sonata he'd written and dedicated to Eli. She hadn't forgiven him for embarrassing her (his dedication was as sappy as *American Idol*). Besides, Eli was with Eric now. Frankly, I preferred Jack and his brooding dark genius to Eric's in-your-pants extraversion. But Eli had made her choice.

Or had she? When Jack said, "Hey, Eli," my dear, unflappable friend seemed to squirm a bit on the bench.

She said, "We'll be out of here in a minute."

Jack approached the upright. "Don't rush off on my account. I'd like to hear you play."

These two used to play duets together on twin uprights pushed to face each other. They'd look over their sheet music into each other's eyes, their metronomes and heartbeats in unison. They communicated on the level that only musicians (and possibly dogs) could hear—words as notes, chords as phrases, measures as sentences.

Eric was a writer, a word guy. I wondered if he really spoke Eli's language.

She said, "I was just fooling around." Eli began playing "Romeo and Juliet" from the top.

Jack walked behind her to see the music. He said, "May I?"

Eli nodded and he sat next to her, started playing along in a higher octave, embellishing, improvising. They didn't speak at all, just sat next to each other, making something bigger than Eli could have made on her own. Their breathing shallow, their minds engaged. I announced I was leaving. I doubt they heard me.

I put my bag over my shoulder and left them alone. Together. I was only a few steps out of the room when I saw Eric Brainard bombing down the hallway.

I said, "We need to talk. About the Matilda Rossi article. I have a decree from on high—"

"Ms. Ratzenberger?"

"Higher."

"Sondra Fortune?" he asked, in a hushed tone.

I nodded gravely. "She's asked me to ask you not to publish any more articles, photos or reflections about, of or by Matilda Rossi."

Eric, who, as of three months ago, would have genuflected at the mere mention of Sondra's name, said, "You can tell Sondra to dream the fuck on. That cover is an instant classic. I'm the first student editor to publish contemporary journalism at Brownstone. A newspaper that responds to the needs and desires of the people. I'm going to run a weekly photo of Ms. Rossi. From now on."

"The *Brief* is to be Brownstone's version of *Maxim*."

"Bingo."

"What about the needs and desires of the female population?"

"Who cares about them?"

"What?"

"Kidding, Dora. You forget how funny I am. To answer your question, the world of print journalism these days is all about finding a niche. A specific subset of the population that appreciates focused editorial content."

"I get it, Eric," I said. "But the *Brief* already caters to a niche. The students at Brownstone."

"I'm going for a smaller core."

"More like a rotten core," I said.

Eric ignored that. "Have you seen Eli?" he asked. "She said she'd be down here."

I'd sworn to Eli three months ago that I would never interfere with her romantic life again. And it wasn't that I was so high on Jack Carp, whom I'd always found mysterious and remote. I understood Eric better, but I liked him less.

I said, "I just checked the music room for her myself. No one in there except Jack Carp."

Eric bristled at the mention of Jack's name. He said, "If you see her, tell her I was looking."

I nodded, and waited to make sure he left the area. Eli and Jack should have one single afternoon together. I flipped open my cell to call Noel and tell him what I'd just done, but then I remembered. Beat love down. Love is not tender. If Noel wanted to talk, he would call me. I snapped the phone closed.

Then I opened it and called. His cell rang and rang. His voice mail picked up.

I said, "Hi, Noel. My parents are going out tonight with some old friend of Dad's. They've been fighting about it for days, which I would have told you about, had you called. Anyway, I was wondering if you'd like to come over tonight. Joya might be around, but she's been locking herself in her room lately. My point, which seems only too obvious by now, is that we'd have complete privacy. We could—" *BEEP*.

I got cut off. I didn't call back. Figured he'd get the message.

Eleven

Mom said, "We'll be home by ten."

"Or a little after," said Dad.

Mom looked at me and repeated, "Ten o'clock."

"No rush," I sang. "Stay out. Have a few drinks. Catch up with your old friend. Who sounds like a fascinating woman. Metallurgist. Olympic skier. Hand model."

"She also writes political poetry and plays the sitar."

I pretended to be impressed. Mom said, "She also borrowed five thousand dollars from your father, used it to move to Paris. Twenty years ago. At a time in our lives when five thousand was a huge amount of money. To this day, I get angry at Ed for giving it to her."

"I didn't know she'd disappear," Dad said in his defense.

"Why do it at all?" I asked. "If you were so hard up, why lend so much cash to a friend?"

Mom stared at Dad. She also would like to know. Dad shrugged helplessly.

Mom said, "He won't admit he was manipulated by Patty. She played him like a glockenspiel. Which is to say, hammered at him with a soft mallet until he gave her whatever she wanted."

"Did you have sex with her?" I asked.

Mom and Dad said, "Dora!"

"Did you? If you gave her five thousand dollars, I hope you got something in return."

Mom snorted. "If he'd had sex with Patty, all he'd get was a raging STD."

Dad said, "Patty was a friend. Just a friend."

Mom said, "Some friend. Steals our money, leaves the country and never contacts us again."

"Until now," said Dad. "Maybe she's going to pay back the loan."

"Twenty years later?" asked Mom. "What about two decades' worth of compound interest?"

"I hadn't realized you were so mercenary, Mom," I said.

"I don't care about the money," she snapped. "It's the principle of the thing."

Dad rolled his eyes. I winked at him. Mom might care about the principle of the thing. But she really cared about the money.

Joya came down the stairs, gloomy, lead of foot, heavy of heart. She said, "I'm leaving."

I did the happy dance. That would mean Noel and I would have the place to ourselves.

"Can we give you a lift?" asked Dad.

"I can walk," said Joya. "Ben is only a few blocks away."

My sister usually skipped out the door when she was off to see Ben. Maybe they'd had a fight.

"Don't hurry back," I said to her.

"Are you expecting company, Dora?" asked Mom, her advice-giving sensors on high alert.

"Noel might come by," I said casually.

"Patty O'Hearn!" blurted Dad. "I still can't believe she called. I wonder if she's as beautiful now as she was twenty years ago."

Mom, Joya and I blinked at Dad. Sometimes he blurted the stupidest things.

"Ten o'clock," said Mom.

Where the hell was Noel? I'd had the place to myself for an hour already, and he hadn't shown up, called, texted or e-mailed. Granted, we hadn't confirmed the plan. He'd never acknowledged my kind offer to *BEEP* at my place.

If he blew me off—again—after I'd been beeping explicit about what he could expect tonight, that would be the biggest insult he could possibly give me. It'd be unforgivable. A relationship ender. A friendship buster, too. I'd have to stare through him every day at school for the next year and a half. Since my eyes were usually unconsciously drawn immediately to him, pretending he was invisible would be a challenge.

And I still didn't know what I'd done to so horribly offend him. I'd sidestepped a few alone-together offers. I'd been jealous. But that hardly seemed like reason enough to strike a deadly relationship blow.

My thoughts, surely, would have continued to darken had they not been interrupted by the stuttering buzz of our intercom.

"Thank God. He's here." I exhaled.

I buzzed him through the two front doors. I heard the thump of footsteps coming up the three flights. I had that long to steady my breath and calm my thundering heart. To be completely honest, I felt more relief than excitement, a raw emotional reaction that I would scrutinize later, when I was (all) alone.

A polite knock. I swung the door open, smiling, eager. Dare I say, *ready*.

Matt Greene, sun-kissed and shimmering, filled the doorway with his radiance. He asked, "Do you take walk-ins?"

I glanced over his shoulder. Where was Noel?

He added, "I hope it's not too late. I come with news from my mother. Actually, a poem. By Lord Byron. She wants the bridesmaids to recite it at the wedding."

I continued to process the turn of events. Matt Greene— *not* Noel Kepner—had come to relieve me of my loneliness. As substitutes went, Matt was no slouch. In fact, he stood straight, tall, strong, smiling and waiting patiently with slightly raised eyebrows.

I said, "A wedding poem? 'Roses are red, violets smell nice; Stephanie likes to marry, so she's doing it twice.' "

Matt laughed. "Good. Next time, though, make it a dirty limerick."

I said, "Please come in."

As Matt stepped into our apartment, he said, "Nice place you have here. Is your family around? I'd love to say hello to Gloria and Ed. And Joya, of course."

The last time Matt had seen Joya she was just ten years old, a runty fifth grader. We were sitting on the stoop at our old building on Hicks Street—me, Joya, Liza and Eli—watching Matt and Ryan Greene pack their possessions into a rented van. Ryan was moving to Bermuda; Matt was going to college. The day she lost the men in her life, Liza was inconsolable. Stephanie cried for her daughter and herself. Joya cried, too. Not made of stone, I also welled a bit. It was a veritable fjord of tears on Hicks Street that day. Only Eli managed to hold it together and comfort Liza, assuring her that she still had us, her surrogate sisters.

Liza said, "But we don't live together." Indeed, by then, our family and Eli's had moved from Hicks Street to bigger apartments. "It's the day in, day out breathing the same oxygen in the same space that makes a family," she wailed into Eli's embrace.

Joya and I made eye contact, seeing in each other's faces the images of our parents. Mom in hers, Dad in mine. Not to discount Eli's bond with her adopted parents. Or the deep connections between friends. On that day, on the stoop, Ryan and Matt leaving Brooklyn in a van, Eli and Liza hugging a step below, I was jolted by the electric surge of shared DNA between Joya and me. No matter how close I was to my friends, I'd always be closer to her. Blood was binding. Even when it was congealed and clotty.

Matt removed his winter coat. I said, "My parents went into the city and Joya's on a date."

"Joya can't date," he said. "She's ten years old."

"She's fourteen," I corrected. "You probably think I'm still thirteen."

Matt shook his head and said, "Not by a long shot, Dora."

I gulped. "Would you like something to drink? Water? Diet Coke? My throat is suddenly Mojave dry." I led him into our black and white kitchen and opened the fridge.

"Got any beer?" he asked.

"Dad isn't much of a beer guy," I said, apologizing. "He pretends to know about wine, but his expertise begins and ends with Zinfandel is Californian, Bordeaux is French."

"That's about as much as I know," said Matt, reaching over my shoulder (he was so *tall*) and grabbing a can of Diet Coke. He had to lean in close, and his chest brushed against my back.

"We used to be in and out of each others' apartments and refrigerators," he remembered. "Your dad and Bertram Stomp treated me like the son they never had—to put to hard labor.

Do you have any idea how many bags of groceries I carried up those stairs? Or how many bulky packages I had to haul around? Being the only boy in the building wasn't a blessing. My muscles ache just thinking about rearranging Anita Stomp's furniture."

I got a Diet Coke and turned around to face him. "Sometimes, when I'm distracted, I find myself walking to Hicks Street instead of Garden Place," I admitted.

The fridge door still open, Matt stepped forward, forcing me to step back. My butt pressed against the crisper drawer.

"And what distracts you, Dora?" asked Matt, bending down, his face only inches from mine.

The can slid out of my hand and crashed to the floor.

Without taking his blue eyes off me, he said, "You dropped your Coke."

"I know."

"Don't open it or it'll spray everywhere."

"I won't."

"So what's the story with you and Noel Kepner?" he asked.

"I'm not sure."

"Be my date to the wedding." He stated it more than asked.

"Okay," I said without hesitating. "Why are you so tan?"

"I'm just back from Bermuda. Visiting Dad."

"It looks good," I said. "Really good."

He smiled, leaned in closer. It would have been sexy as hell, but my ass was going numb. "I could have e-mailed the poem," he said.

"The dirty limerick? 'There once was a bride from Nantucket'?"

He nodded. "Much as I wanted to see your family, I'm glad they're not here."

And then he kissed me, without asking first, as Brownstone boys had been trained to do, lest they risk being accused of sexual harassment. The "ask first" policy must have been before Matt's time. He dove into my lips like they were a swimming pool. The idea that I might have an objection hadn't entered his consciousness.

I was at once offended and seduced by his confidence. The fact that his lips tasted like mint balm and that his tongue was warm and smooth added to the seduction part. If the refrigerator thermostat hadn't kicked into high gear, we might have stood there forever, until my butt froze onto the crisper drawer.

Matt pulled back, and I opened my eyes. I knew exactly whom I'd been kissing, but I was nonetheless amazed to see Matt Greene, Liza's brother, and all his radiance shining down at me.

He said, "I always liked you, Dora. Even when you had braces."

"I never liked you, Matt," I said, as he pulled me away from the fridge.

"I was a jerk," he agreed. "I spied on you girls. I have seen you naked. When you were seven."

"You filthy pervert!" I shrieked.

"It's been ten years," he said. "Perhaps you'd like to refresh my memory."

"Dream on, college boy," I said, smiling.

"Why are we in the kitchen?" he asked.

"To the living room," I said. "Away!"

We dashed though the dining room and, with the good running start, flung ourselves onto the living room couch like we had as kids. We landed in a tangle, giggling. Matt lifted me onto his lap. I slid off. I was attracted to him (and how), but I wasn't ready for serious snogging. Just because I'd known him my whole life didn't mean he wasn't a stranger now.

He moved in for a smack, and I pushed his face away. He could take a subtle hint.

"Do you have any thoughts about colleges?" he asked gamely.

"I'm ignoring my future," I said.

He nodded. "That might work," he said. "Temporarily."

It was louder all the time, the chatter in the upper school hallways about SATs and college applications. A lot of the pressure came from parents. But the tightest screws came from other students. At Brownstone, peer pressure was about getting high scores and good grades, not smoking and drinking. Anyone who wasn't desperate to get into an Ivy was considered a crazy rebel. It was the effete Brooklyn private school equivalent of shaving one's head and shooting heroin.

I said, "Eli's the one with her eyes on the prize." Harvard. "Liza says she wants to move to Bermuda and run snorkel boat tours with your dad."

"She could do worse," said Matt. "A father who chucked

it all to live on an island might not be the best role model. But when things get tough, he's a built-in escape plan. The question is, What would Liza be escaping from?" I gave him the "duh" expression. "Yes, of course," he said. "Gary."

"I try, but I just can't get myself to care too much about the 'right' college."

"What does Noel Kepner want?" asked Matt, his eyes flickering over me. "For his future?"

If Noel had a grand plan, he hadn't shared it with me. Granted, I hadn't asked. It would be just a little awkward. Him: "Wanna go to Grind for lunch?" Me: "What are your deepest hopes and dreams?" Besides that, if I asked him, he'd ask me back. The fantasies I had of my future were so predictable that I embarrassed myself when I had them.

"Noel's long- or short-term plans do not include me, if that's what you're asking." I felt an oncoming salty wave of sadness. "He was supposed to come over tonight. As you see, he didn't. I knew he'd dump me sooner than later. He changes girlfriends like T-shirts. But I thought he'd have the courtesy to let me know he was done with me."

I cried. Just a little. The hurt was real. Matt Greene gave me a tight hug. "I'm a shit for kissing you," he said. "I didn't realize this was fresh."

"It's not fresh," I corrected. "It's raw."

He stroked my hair and assured me, "Noel is an idiot. Deserves to be strung up by the tender parts. He's making the biggest mistake of his sorry life."

I sobbed and sniveled. "You're just saying that to be nice."

Toying with a lock of my hair, he said, "The best way to get over a breakup is to start seeing someone new."

The apartment door swung open and boots stomped down the short hallway into the dining room. Matt and I, in our demi-grapple, turned toward the commotion. Joya stood at the table in her coat, hat, muffler, keys swinging from her gloved hand.

She gaped at us like she'd caught us skinning a cat. The shock in her eyes was hardly called for. I figured she was purposely overreacting to pay me back for the incident the other day with Ben.

She opened her mouth to speak, to shout a warning, as I now understood it, but instead a panicked peep warbled out. She started to point at the hallway, the keys jingling in the air.

Matt whispered, "Is that Joya?"

"As far as I can tell."

"What's wrong with her?"

I shook my head. "Where shall I begin?"

We laughed a bit, then stopped cold when another voice bounced into the apartment. "Thanks for letting me up, Joya," it said. "Something must be wrong with the buzzer."

Noel Kepner walked into my dining room casually, as comfortable in my home as he was in his own skin. He stood next to Joya, who was still mute. He was in his socks. He'd apparently removed his boots before entering. A dusting of snow covered the top of his hair. His cheeks were windblown and red. He looked at Joya, confused by her frozen posture, and then he glanced the length of the apartment, into the living room.

What a sight: me huddled against Matt Greene on the couch, his hands around my waist, mine around his neck.

Noel, for perhaps the second time in the twelve years I'd known him, had been rendered speechless.

Joya said, "Noel was waiting on the stoop, so I let him up."

Stating the obvious was one of her special skills. "You didn't call to confirm!" I said lamely to Noel. "This is Matt Greene—Liza's brother, like a brother to me, too. He stopped by and we were just talking."

Noel's eyes, I could see from across the apartment, were glistening and wounded. Also full of male proprietary anger. It was kind of thrilling. In a stomach-lurching kind of way.

Matt reacted first. He said, "Joya, it's great to see you."

"Matt? It is you!" said Joya. She beamed, ran at him and jumped in his arms. These two—both excluded from the threesome of me, Eli and Liza—had formed a bond on Hicks Street. I didn't know what it was, but I knew it existed.

He caught her and laughed. I flashed back to when Joya was around four and Matt was ten, how he would draw princesses and ponies with her when no one else had the patience. Matt had encouraged her artistic aspirations more than anyone else way back when.

Noel watched Joya and Matt's reunion. Out of the corner of my eye, I studied him. He seemed to be barely holding himself back from throttling Matt with his gloved hands.

When Joya and Matt finally let go of each other, I said, "Matt Greene, this is Noel Kepner."

"Hello," said Matt politely, with the ease and sophistication of a college junior. He reached out to shake.

Noel looked down at Matt's hand. I just knew he was going to slap it away in a blind fury.

Noel removed his glove and said, "Hello, Matt. I remember you from Brownstone. Nice to see you again. Aren't you at Northwestern? It must be freezing in Evanston." He took Matt's hand, pumped once and dropped it.

"I'm taking a semester off, actually," said Matt, which I hadn't realized, but it made sense. "For my mom's wedding. And I'm interning with a research team at the Rose Planetarium for my astronomy major."

"Astronomy?" I asked. Not what I considered a sexy major. I wasn't sure what was, but definitely not stars. Jeez. Geology—rocks—at least that had some grit. And, meanwhile, Noel wasn't tearing Matt limb from limb. He was all toothy politeness and genuine curiosity toward the guy he'd just seen in a clench with his girfriend (however estranged and/or erstwhile).

"We're studying *Romeo and Juliet* in English lit," I threw in. "The star-crossed lovers."

Matt and Noel turned toward me, smiling tolerantly.

Noel said, "Yeah." To Matt: "I haven't been to the planetarium in years."

"It's had some major renovations," said Matt.

And then they sat down together at the dining room table and talked for fifteen minutes about the improvements at the Museum of Natural History.

Joya was as baffled as I was by this confounding civility. She pulled me aside and whispered, "Matt's gorgeous."

I said, "I hadn't noticed."

"How could you not," she said, "with your face pressed against his rippling, massive chest?"

"You're back early," I said. "Trouble with Ben?"

Joya blushed. As she removed her outer layers, she said, "Sorry about letting Noel in. We need some kind of system. Like a sock on the door."

The last thing I wanted to discuss with my flat-chested sister was a code for sexual opportunism.

"I can think of another place to put a sock," I muttered. Then, more loudly, "Since the two of you are getting along so famously, I'll just go upstairs and read a book."

The men stopped talking about the prehistoric wing and turned their attention to me—where it rightfully belonged. Matt said, "I was just leaving. Thanks for the Coke, Dora. Great to see you, Joya."

"Will you come over again?" she asked eagerly. "I've got so much to tell you, and show you. I've drawn some graphic novellas. A lot of it is based on the stuff we did together. It's called 'Lake Monster Barbie Finds Love and Dies. Parts One and Two.' She doesn't really die. She's undead."

Matt seemed touched. "I'd love to see them."

"Okay!" she said, stomping upstairs to get her sketchbook before Matt could object.

Noel said, "I need to push along, too."

"You just got here," I said.

"It's getting ugly out there," he said, pointing toward the dining room window. Marry, it was. The snow was heavy. The night sky was white, fluttering, falling.

Joya thundered downstairs with a couple of her sketchbooks. She found a plastic bag and wrapped them so Matt could take them safely home in the snow.

While they were busy, I brushed my knuckles on the back of Noel's hand. He flinched, as if I'd scalded him.

It was getting ugly in here, too.

I said, "You didn't confirm."

"You had Matt Greene on standby?" he asked coldly.

"Why didn't you call all weekend?"

"I was angry with you," he said. "You don't trust me."

"I do trust you!" I protested.

He said, "You should."

"What, so now you don't trust me?" I asked.

Pointing his chin at Matt, he said, "I guess I don't."

"You're just looking for an excuse to end it," I said.

He said, "If you say so."

"Are *you* saying so?" I asked. This was maddening. "Let's speak plainly, Noel. Are you putting me on warning? Am I on romantic probation?"

"I'm breaking up with you," he said.

Twelve

"You've reached Dora Benet. At the sound of the zoink, please start speaking. *ZOINK*," I said into my cell. I was at my locker when it chirped. One day post-Noel. I think I was still numb from the shock.

"Fringe," said the voice.

"Sondra?" I asked. "You have my cell number?"

"Meet me at Monty's at lunch today," she commanded. "And don't be late."

She hung up. I flipped my phone shut, and looked down the hallway in the direction of Sondra's locker. There she stood, her phone in her hand. Lori and Micha Dropov, the evil twins, were to her left and right, respectively and respectfully. Sondra glanced in my direction. I gave her a cutesy half wave and the internationally recognized "call me" thumb and pinkie mime.

She sneered from twenty feet away. For Sondra, a little sneer goes a long way.

I had an interview with the queen. And a secret one at that. I was honored, flattered. Afraid. What could she possibly want with Fringe-Dwelling me? The possibilities were endlessly terrifying.

Liza appeared at my locker. I said, "Hello, you, you, you."

" 'We grew apart,' you said. Bull! I know the truth about why you and Noel broke up," Liza announced. "Noel told Stanley and Stanley told me that you and my brother were making out on your couch last night," she said. "I told Stanley that you would never do that to Noel, or to me, since you know that I need Matt's attention right now, because I'm going through some serious shit with my mom, and that you, unlike her, are not a me, me, me selfish bitch."

"I was not making out with your brother!" I said, slamming my locker closed. I was flat-out lying. And I had only just gotten started.

Liza said, "Good. You should defend yourself, Dora. Tell Stanley the truth at lunch today. Just the three of us. We need a mediator, Dora. And Stanley wants you."

"Ohh, lunch today," I said, shaking my head. "No good. I've got a . . . teacher conference. How about after school?"

She frowned. "That won't work. Stanley and I are going to Noel's to read lines."

"In *Romeo and Juliet*?" I asked. "Without me?" It was a verbal kick in the gut. So that was how Noel wanted to play it. Exclude me, purposely leave me friendless. Liza, on the wrong side of the train wreck.

Seeing my hurt expression, Liza said, "I'll talk to him."

"Even when he stopped calling, even when he didn't show up last night—until he did—I thought he just wanted to take a pause. A rest. A comma. But he's really at the end. It's a period for him. A big, black dot."

Panic rose in my chest, burning and suffocating. And then, in the miasma of dread and sickness, Matt Greene's face floated into my head, his minty lips moving, asking about my future.

I said, "Since you won't be needing him this afternoon, perhaps I'll give Matt a call."

Liza frowned (with her eyes, too) and warned, "Stay away from my brother."

Eli caught up with me when I was halfway out the front door at lunchtime to meet Sondra. I was wrapped up in five layers, and I already felt the chill to my marrow. Grabbing my down-padded elbow, Eli dragged me back into the lobby of Brownstone, probably to yell at me for upsetting Liza in her time of great need (which seemed perpetual).

"What did you say to Eric yesterday afternoon?" Eli demanded.

Eric? "I thought you were going to yell at me for what I said to Liza."

"I have that to look forward to," said Eli. "You told Eric that you hadn't seen me, when in fact you'd left a warm spot on my piano bench not two minutes before."

Oh, yeah. Now I remembered. It was right after he said

he didn't give a shit about the female population of Brownstone, with the exception of Ms. Matilda Rossi. "He pissed me off."

"Eric found me alone in the music room with Jack Carp."

"So?" I asked. "Was anything happening?"

"We were making beautiful music together."

"How beautiful?" I asked. "How together?"

Eli said, "What have you got against Eric?"

"He's starting to be a bit top-heavy, if you know what I mean."

"Top-heavy," repeated Eli.

"An inflated ego," I explained. "A massive swelling of the frontal lobes. The guy's gone power-of-the-press mad, Eli."

"And only you can recognize power madness in others."

She was referring to my relentless climb to the top of the social heap the previous term. She was right: Power had corrupted me. "You aren't offended that he wants to turn the *Brief* into *Matilda Rossi Weekly*?"

"It's an experiment!" said Eli, defending him.

I shook my head. "I'm sorry. If you want Eric Brainard, you can have him."

"I don't need your permission," she said and walked away.

After trudging through the wind and snow, I was grateful for the heat of Monty's brick-oven pizza joint. I picked my way toward the rear of the restaurant, weaving through the crowd of lunchtime customers—adults, working people who had no idea of what really happened in the back room at Monty's on school days.

Taking a deep breath, I got to the door, knocked twice. It opened. Lori Dropov stood inside the private dining room, reserved for parties, otherwise used by Sondra Fortune for her top-secret meetings and conferences.

Lori checked for witnesses, then closed the door behind me. The room was dimly lit, with several round tables with classic Italian white and red checkerboard-pattern tablecloths. In the center of each table sat salt, pepper, Parmesan, garlic shakers and a silver napkin dispenser. Sondra sat at the farthest table, in a corner, her back to the wall. Micha Dropov was at her left. A plum-tomato-and-mozzarella slice and an espresso cup were on the table in front of her.

I said, "Hunger."

Sondra snapped her fingers. "Lori. Would you mind terribly getting Adora something to eat? It'd be such a huge favor and I'd really appreciate it."

Instantly, my radar started flashing. Not only was Sondra permitting, nay, encouraging me to eat in her presence, she'd called me by my name. She hadn't taunted me with "Fringe."

Lori said, "Why do I have to get it? The line is so freaking long."

"Micha, go with her. Clearly, she needs help."

Micha seemed startled to be summarily dismissed. She said, "Who's paying?"

Sondra reached into her purse and removed a five from her wallet. The gesture made all of us freeze where we stood and/or sat. Sondra was permitting me to eat *and paying for* my food. This was big.

Micha got up and walked toward Lori at the door. I cringed at the sight of her painfully thin body. "Why don't you get something for yourself?" I suggested.

Sondra said, "Good idea. Stay out there a while."

The Dropovs' lips flapped in mute protest, but then they left us alone.

"You must be suffocating under all those things!" said Sondra, still in dangerously nice mode. "Take off your coat, Adora. Relax."

Suspicious, I said, "Not sure that's possible." I removed unnecessary clothing and ventured closer to her table. I said, "Why does this remind me of a scene from *The Sopranos*? A backroom scene. The boss is always super nice right before he stabs you in the eye."

Sondra laughed and trilled, "Sit next to me."

I'd been invited not only into her lair but also into the Chair? The spot to her right? The second seat of power? Oh, shit! Whatever she wanted, it had to be bad.

I slid into the seat, barely warm from Micha's bony ass. Sondra flashed me one of her brightest, dimpliest trademark smiles. If I were a stranger on the street and I saw that wedge of shiny teeth and glossy lips, I would think she was as friendly as she was beautiful.

But I wasn't a stranger. And that wasn't a smile. She was baring her teeth.

"What can I do for you, Sondra?" I asked.

The smile faded. "You're right," she said. "Of all the people at Brownstone, you're the only one I shouldn't bother pretending to. I have a problem. I need your help."

At the height of our battle last term, Sondra had confessed some personal things to me in the girls' bathroom in the downstairs gym. Things she might not have told anyone else, ever. Even though she'd plotted to destroy me and steal my boyfriend, she had also trusted me with her secrets. Only me.

"This is about Vin?" I asked, speaking of her boyfriend, the one she stole from me.

She nodded. "He's obsessed with Matilda Rossi. He follows her around school. He put a picture of her on his desktop. When we're . . . together . . . I can tell he's not with me. He's there, but not there. You know what I mean?"

"Oh, yeah," I said knowingly. "I completely understand."

Sondra rolled her mascara eyes. "He's thinking about her, okay? I can tell."

I nervously cleared my throat. My sexual inexperience was as plain as my face. "Again, I humbly ask: What can I do for you?"

"Find the chink in Rossi's armor," said Sondra. "Get me some reason, any good reason, to get her booted out of Brownstone."

"You want me to dig dirt on Rossi."

"If you don't mind. I'd appreciate it ever so much."

"What makes you think I'd know the first thing about doing this? I read a lot of mystery novels, but that hardly qualifies me—"

"All you need to dig dirt, Dora, is a shovel," she said.

"I don't have a shovel," I said. "I do realize you're going for metaphor."

Sondra sighed. "Just poke around her office. Get her references from Ms. Ratzenberger's files. See where it takes you."

"Purposely put myself in potentially risky situations."

"Exactly."

"And what makes you think I'd agree to this?" I asked.

"I'd consider it a personal favor. I'll make it up to you," she said.

It would be a good distraction from the mess of my romantic life. "Let me think about it for the day."

She nodded. Business done, she got personal. "By the way, I'm sorry to hear about you and Noel."

Sympathy from the devil herself. Weird how I almost started crying uncontrollably. Thankfully, Micha and Lori banged back in and presented my slice like a birthday present, which sucked my tears back into their ducts. They looked at Sondra expectantly, waiting for her approval. She graced them with it. "Thanks, guys."

"What'd we miss?" asked Lori.

Sondra said, "Nothing. Just comparing notes."

The evil twins glanced at each other. They knew she was holding out on them. Suspicion flitted over their sharp-boned faces. And then, an emotion I was all too familiar with in the context of Sondra Fortune: rank, abject fear.

Thirteen

A Brooklyn Winter's Tale
Week III, Scene I
English lit classroom, Wednesday morning

Ms. Rossi as Juliet clutched a hankie to the plunging V of her neckline. She said, " 'As sweet repose and rest come to thy heart, as that within my breast.' "

Freddy Pluto, the class idiot, coughed. "She said 'breast.' "

A gentle zephyr of titters followed. Ms. Rossi said, "Noel. Pray, continue."

" 'O, wilt thou leave me so unsatisfied?' " recited Noel as Romeo.

Freddy coughed and said, "Blue balls."

Ms. Rossi said, " 'What satisfaction canst thou have to-night?' "

Freddy added, "Cock tease." Noel looked right at me.

Bastard.

" 'The exchange of thy love's faithful vow for mine,' " he recited as Romeo.

Ms. Rossi lowered her book. "Can anyone tell me what is happening in this scene? How about . . . Liza Greene?"

My friend's blond head snapped to attention at the mention of her name. She stammered, "Uh, well, they're talking about how much they love each other."

"Obviously, Liza," said Ms. Rossi condescendingly. "Can you possibly delve any deeper than that?"

Liza's eyes welled (like mother, like daughter), and both Stanley Nable and I started grinding our teeth. What was it about Liza that made me so protective? I could be furious at her, but I'd still fling my body between her and a chain saw.

"What's happening in the scene," I said, speaking out of turn, "is that Romeo is demanding reassurance from Juliet, and she's gently putting him off. He's very insecure. And he could be dangerous. I mean, she just met the guy, and he's declaring his undying love? He followed her home like a stalker. They exchanged like four sentences before he kissed her—without asking, by the way, which violates the established Brownstone code of conduct. If Romeo were a student at this school, he'd be hauled into the staff shrink's office for sexual harassment."

Freddy Pluto said, "She said 'ass.' "

"Please SHUT UP," said Ms. Rossi to him.

Noel said, "So you think Romeo's asking for reassurance is a sign of insecurity? You think that a boy should be able to read a girl's mind? Is that how relationships work for you, Dora? Telepathically?"

"Let's see if you can figure out what I'm thinking right now," I said and gave Noel a very hairy eyeball.

He said, "You're wondering how a relationship that started with such promise could go so wrong, so fast."

Ouch. Dagger words. To the throat.

Ms. Rossi said, "Good point, Noel. The span of *Romeo and Juliet* is only four days. Enough time to fall in love, get married, be separated, and reunite only to die in each other's arms."

I said, "I have to go to the bathroom."

Ms. Rossi waved me toward the door. She was happy to get rid of me. It was only a few minutes before the end of the class, so I gathered my stuff. I moved fast, rushing to escape the suffocating room before Noel saw me cry. I was halfway out the door when Ms. Rossi said, "See me in my office after school today, Ms. Benet."

Week III, Scene II
The entrance to Chez Brownstone, Wednesday lunchtime

I poked my head in, checking for enemies, and spotted Eli sitting with Eric (not friendly), Liza with Stanley and Noel (likewise). Jack Carp sat by himself at the end of a long table, his earphones on, completely absorbed in what he was listening to. Hence, he probably wouldn't care to listen to me, even if we spoke the same language, which we don't.

I took my lonesome self to Grind, where I could jump into a latte and drown. I wasn't a block away from school when, as I turned the corner on Joralemon Street, a bony claw reached out and grabbed my shoulder, pulling me into the cranny under the stoop of a building.

Slamming me against an iron gate, my captor said, "Okay, Dora, what the hell is going on with you and Sondra?"

Micha Dropov, all ninety pounds of her, snarled at me viciously. Her sister, Lori, scowled behind her. I said, "For a skinny minny, you've got quite a grip." Micha's talons would leave bruises on my arm.

"Is it about us?" asked Lori. "She wants to dump us, doesn't she?"

I rubbed my elbow and said, "At present, I'm not able to divulge the details of my meeting with Sondra. But it doesn't have anything to do with you."

"Liar!" spat Lori, the smaller (weighing in at eighty-eight pounds, all of it taut ballerina) and more sinister of the pair.

"Wait, I get it. This is a test," I said. "Sondra sent you to rough me up, see if I'll spill?"

The evil twins considered going with that, but decided (out of character) to be honest. "She won't talk to us anymore," whined Micha. "Ever since she's been with Vin, Sondra's been acting funny."

"How so?"

"She doesn't want to hang out at her apartment, eat Krispy

Kremes and trash other girls," said Lori. "She refuses to go shopping, and she hasn't hatched a plot to humiliate a random loser for months."

"It's all Vin Transom, all the time," sniffed Micha. "I don't see the attraction. He's got a great runner's body, but he barely speaks! The guy might as well be verbally challenged. And the way he dresses! He never saw a pair of cargo pants he didn't like. He hangs out with the zitty idiots on the track team. I gag in their general direction. Sondra could do a million times better."

Lori nodded along. "She's lowering herself to be with him," she added succinctly.

It was no surprise to me that Sondra had cooled on the twins. They hated her boyfriend. To Sondra's credit, she *had* lowered herself to be with Vin, if only in the social hierarchy at Brownstone. Vin was of the Teeming Masses; Sondra was queen of the Ruling Class. She'd jumped down two rungs to be with him. If we were in ancient Rome, it'd be like a patrician dating a plebeian, which was practically illegal.

"Has it occurred to either one of you that Sondra might actually be in love with Vin? That she's willing to sacrifice her standing, her friends and her strict style requirements because she loves the guy?"

The twins squinted at me, confused. Micha asked, "What is this *love* of which you speak?"

"Impossible," said Lori. "No way she could care that much about a loser like Vin. Ergo, she's dumping us. And you're involved."

She got a mad Russian glare in her eyes, and I felt a genuine chill, like she might come for me in the night and throw me in the gulag. Time to make myself gone.

I gingerly inched my way around their scrawny blockade. "It's been great catching up," I said. "Let's do it again real soon. Sometime next decade."

Lori pointed two fingers at her eyes and then directed them at mine. The international code for "I'm watching you." And I knew she would. Like an anorexic hawk.

Week III, Scene III
Stairway to hell, Wednesday after school

The line of boys waiting to enter Ms. Rossi's impromptu office snaked all the way down the stairs and halfway along the east wall of Chez Brownstone.

I considered getting in the back of the line. But then, unlike these pathetic fans of Ms. Rossi's, I'd been invited, summoned, ordered, whatever. Using a gentle elbow, I pushed my way up the stairs, through the press of horny underclassmen, and barged into the Forbidden Zone.

Ms. Rossi sat like a head of state behind her desk. Her laptop was open, casting a ghostlike glow on her porcelain skin, which I, for one, found unattractive.

Standing behind her desk, over her shoulder, slightly to her right, Eric Brainard grinned at me sophomorically, even though he was a senior.

I approached the desk. "Here I am," I said.

Ms. Rossi kept her eyes on the screen. "I'm nearly done here," she said. "Okay, Eric. It looks good. I made some notations, but otherwise you can go ahead."

Raising my brows, I went for a look of intellectual curiosity. "Oh? Will you be writing for the *Brief*?"

"Eric has asked me to write an advice column," she said. "Readers supply the questions, and I—"

"I'm familiar with the format."

Eric said, "Dora's parents write a Q-and-A advice column in the *New York Moon*," he said. "It's syndicated all over the country." If only Eli could see her boyfriend now, scraping like a coolie for Ms. Rossi's pleasure.

Ms. Rossi squinted at me. "Your parents are Gloria and Ed Benet? Authors of *His-and-Her Divorce*, *His-and-Her Dating*, and *His-and-Her Seduction*?"

God help me, was Ms. Rossi a *fan*? "Currently reporting and writing *His-and-Her Romance*," I said, dutifully plugging their upcoming tome.

"Perhaps they should try writing *His-and-Her Parenting*," she sneered obnoxiously. "If your behavior in class is any indication of how they've raised you, your parents could stand to do some research on where they went wrong."

The woman turned toward Eric, stroked him three times up and down his forearm and said, "Can't wait to see the column in the *Brief* tomorrow."

Beads of sweat forming on his upper lip, he said, "I'm grateful for the opportunity to publish your thoughts and ideas."

I gagged. Couldn't help it.

Ms. Rossi said, "Eric, you may go. Unfortunately, I have less pleasant matters to deal with now."

Eric had been dismissed. He nodded, clicked his sneaker heels and walked out backward, bowing as he went. At the door, he had to push through the clamoring boys who fought for a glimpse inside.

Ms. Rossi closed her laptop and asked me to sit in the chair in front of her desk. I did. She said, "Since you have writer parents, I'm surprised by your obvious disinterest in literature."

"I love *literature*," I corrected. "I hate you." Okay, I didn't really say that last part. I thought it. Loud.

Ms. Rossi said, "Your behavior in class is hostile and disruptive. Whatever your personal problems are with Noel Kepner, if you can't keep them out of my classroom, I'm going to send a warning notification to Ms. Ratzenberger."

Warning notification was the first step in the lengthy process of kicking a kid out of school. After the warning, a teacher could send a second warning and then issue a failing grade, which meant automatic probation and potential expulsion for academic ineptitude. I wish I were kidding. At fancy private schools in New York City, including Brooklyn Heights, standards were sky-high. One bad grade and your entire life was thrown into turmoil. Teachers usually bent over backward to help kids in trouble and avoid the bloody carnage of an expulsion. But those other teachers had what Ms. Rossi lacked: a beating human heart.

"Just because I spoke in class without raising my hand?" I was flabbergasted. "Seems a tad extreme."

"You don't like me, do you?" she asked flatly. "You hate me. You curse my name in bed at night." Ms. Rossi laughed mockingly. "There's a girl like you in every school. A paranoid, jealous brat who thinks she's ten times smarter than she really is. I've let girls like you make trouble for me before. But not this time. I like this neighborhood. And I like this school. I intend to stay. So if you give me one more eye roll, one more cheeky comment, I'll bring the hammer down. Hard."

I'd never been threatened before, not by someone who could do me actual damage. Sondra Fortune had made my life difficult, but not in a way that could jeopardize my "future." Ms. Rossi was older than I was. She was in a power position. I didn't stand a chance against her. I was vulnerable, defenseless, shocked—and fascinated. This was new. This feeling of being attacked unjustly, it made my pulse race. I kinda liked it.

"You're saying, 'This school ain't big enough for both of us.' Correct?" I asked.

She nodded gravely, her blue eyes an eerie shade of menace. "That's right, Dora. It's you or me."

"In that case, I choose you," I said. "You, you, you."

Smiling, she said, "Maybe you're smarter than I thought."

"Now that we have that straightened out," I said, "tell me, are you or are you not flirting with Noel Kepner, Vin Transom—even Eric Brainard?"

"Flirting?" she sneered. "I'm twenty-nine years old, Dora. I don't flirt."

So she was twelve years older than me. She'd told Eric Brainard she was twenty-six (vain, too). "I'm only asking to fully understand why you've threatened me: You do or do not find Noel Kepner attractive?"

"Get out of my face, and never speak to me on a personal level again."

"All rightie, then," I said. I zipped my lips and threw away the key and speed-walked the hell out of there.

Vin Transom had pushed his way to the front of the line of boys outside.

I flipped open my cell and dialed.

"Fringe," said Sondra, picking up on the first ring.

"I'll do it."

Fourteen

"Preparation is to success as okra is to gumbo," said Mrs. Strombone on Saturday morning. "Who wants to try one? Dora? Feeling perkier this week?"

Another woman who picked on me. "The thing is, Mrs. Strombone—all due respect, gratitude and supplication—the verbal section of the SATs doesn't include analogies anymore," I said.

She laughed. "Humor is to defense mechanism as . . . Eli Stomp? Want to give it a go?"

"Dora's right, Mrs. Strombone," ventured Eli. She spoke politely. Softly.

"Speak up."

"She said I was right." I spoke for Eli, who was way too polite to the elderly to tell it like it was. "The college board changed the SAT test years ago and dropped analogies. The emphasis now is on reading comprehension and writing."

"Writing?" Mrs. Strombone's lips had gone Elmer's white.

"Eight hundred points of your score is based on essay writing," I said.

"Half the score?" Mrs. Strombone whispered reverently.

"A third," I replied. "The total number of points now is twenty-four hundred."

"Two thousand and four ... they can't *do* that. Who knew about these changes? All of you? And you let me go on and on about analogies? Ohhhh, my heart!" The old woman clutched her chest and stumbled backward, crashing into her chalkboard, knocking it to the floor and then collapsing on top of it.

The three St. Andrews boys responded immediately, jumping out of their chairs—and then running out of the room with their backpacks and coats.

Cowards.

Liza screamed, "Call 911! Call 911! Someone call—" I threw my phone at her. "I'll do it!" she volunteered.

Eli and I dashed over to Mrs. Strombone, flat on her back, fists gripping the lace collar of her dress. Her ancient eyes were open and moving, bouncing from Eli's face to mine. Her paste-white lips trembled.

"You're a doctor's daughter," I yelled at Eli. "Do something."

"I don't know what to do!"

"Something must have filtered through by osmosis," I insisted. "Check her pulse. Give her mouth-to-mouth."

" 'Come take an SAT class in the basement of Mrs. Strombone's house,' you said," Eli mocked. " 'It'll be fun,' you said."

"Isn't this fun?" I asked in a panic.

"She's clearly breathing," said Eli, pointing at Mrs. Strombone's heaving bosom.

Liza, meanwhile, was screaming into the phone. "A woman is dying! She might already be dead!"

Mrs. Strombone thrashed frantically at the news that she might already be dead.

"Definitely not dead," I said.

"Mrs. Strombone," said Eli, "we're here for you. Can I get you a glass of water?"

Her withered mouth trembled. She was trying to say something. Eli and I leaned down, straining to hear what might be her final words on earth.

"What is it, Mrs. Strombone?" I asked. She was struggling, desperate to speak, confess some old secret. "You had a child out of wedlock and gave him to the nuns? You had an affair with your husband's best friend? Once, years ago, you killed a man?"

She nodded, then shook her head. "You *have* killed a man?" I asked. "The body's buried somewhere here? Under the floorboards?"

"Oh my God," said Eli. "She's pointing."

A trembling finger, right at my nose. My throat constricted. Once, years ago, she killed *me*? The old woman grunted, forced out words by sheer force of will. "Your mother . . ."

"What?"

"Your mother . . ."

"Yes?!"

With her last iota of strength, Mrs. Strombone said, "Your mother is going to hear about this and she's not going to like it!"

"I did *not* almost kill Mrs. Strombone," I protested for the tenth time.

"Keep shoveling," said Mom from the top of our stoop, a cup of steaming-hot coffee warming her gloves. "And when you finish the steps, you can do the sidewalk. And you should salt, too. Another storm is coming in."

"Where's global warming when you need it?" I grumbled, digging in deep with the shovel.

"Why do I have to shovel?" asked Joya. "I didn't give Mrs. Strombone a heart attack."

"No, but Martha Teare almost had one last night when she caught you and Ben on their couch!" barked Mom.

I grinned and asked my careless sister, "Don't you learn from your mistakes?"

Joya put her shoulder into it, collecting a huge load of snow from the sidewalk. She said, "Shut up, Dora."

"Or maybe you *want* to be caught," I said. "You *like* the thrill of doing it in public."

"You have a filthy mind," said Joya.

"Wait, I've got it," I said, a realization striking. "It's not that you want to be caught. You want to be *stopped*!" I made sure Mom wasn't listening and whispered, "That's it, isn't it? So much for 'sex as a grand adventure.' So much for 'sex will add dimension to my art.' "

Mom said, "Less talking, more shoveling."

I added, "You're just as chicken as I am, Joya. At least I can admit it."

Joya flung the shovelful at my face. Incredibly, I didn't see it coming at me. My reactions were a bit sluggish since the near death this morning. (Mrs. Strombone survived the attack and was resting comfortably at Long Island College Hospital a few blocks away.)

I brushed snow off my shoulders and said to Mom, "Did you see that?"

Mom said, "See what?" She'd been searching for the meaning of life inside her coffee mug. "Where could your father *be*?"

"I don't think you'll find him in there."

"When's the last time you saw him?" asked Joya as if we were discussing a missing set of car keys.

"He went to the city. He's tracking down that old friend of his," grumbled Mom. "The woman we had dinner with last week? Our business is not yet concluded."

"She gave you a check for five thousand dollars," I said. "You waved it at me like a flag."

"It bounced to the moon," said Mom.

I loaded up my shovel, intending to exact my cold-dish revenge on Joya. But she'd already reloaded, and now she splattered me on the legs, the snow tumbling into my boots. I scooped up a huge ball of the sticky stuff and was on the verge of chucking it when Joya—quick eighth-grade reflexes—pelted me again on my unprotected neck.

Tsking, I shook my head. "We can't bond over a snow fight unless I throw some, too. It's reciprocal. Mutual," I said. "Jesus, do I have to explain everything to you?"

Joya beamed. "We're bonding? Go ahead. Hit me. I'm ready." She closed her eyes and smiled.

"You're ruining it."

"Less bonding," said Mom. "More shoveling."

Ring. Landline? On the stoop? Mom said, "I got it," and took the house phone out of her coat pocket. "Ed?" she asked into it. Pause. Then, "Matt Greene! So sorry we missed you the other night!" she purred. To me and Joya, she said, "It's Matt Greene." Back on the line, she said, "We should all get together for dinner—"

Joya and I both watched Mom as she talked to Matt. He'd obviously called for me, and I pitied him for having to get through the schmooze screen of my mother.

"Matt lusts for you," taunted Joya. "Then again," she added, her pixie eyes twinkling, "maybe he lusts for *me*."

"That would make him a pedophile."

"A party at the Stomps'?" said Mom into the phone. "Tonight? What a fantastic idea! A Hicks Street reunion on Henry Street? What can I bring? I'll have Ed bake a cake." Concern shot across her forehead, remembering Dad was MIA. "At six thirty. Perfect. What? You want to talk to her? She's right here." Mom walked the four steps down the (snow-cleared) stoop, three steps across the (getting there) sidewalk, and held out the phone.

I reached for it, and Mom said, "It's for you . . . *Joya*."

My baby (and I mean it) sister cooed and gurgled. "For me?" She took the phone and held it to her blushing cheek. "Matt? I'm me—JOYA. You read the comics?" She grinned brightly and said, "Really? You mean it? Oh, wait, the line is crackling. Let me go inside."

She continued to gush her gratitude to him as she ran up the stoop steps and into the building. Mom smiled crookedly at me.

"He's humoring her," I said.

"And what's he doing to you?" she asked. "When I handed the phone to Joya, your face nearly fell off."

"Look, I'm very sensitive to the cold, and I'm covered in snow. Am I done?" I asked.

Mom inspected the job, tutting and pecking. "Almost. When you finish here, go shovel Mrs. Strombone's stoop. I told her it'd be clean when she got home from the hospital."

"But I'll just have to do it again if there's another storm," I protested.

"It's up to you," she said, shrugging. "If you don't shovel the stoops, you can't go to the party tonight at Eli's house." She didn't need to add, "where Matt Greene will be."

What could I do? I shoveled the frigging stoop.

Fifteen

"Gary shouldn't be here," said Liza.

The three of us stood in a tight circle by the roaring fireplace in Eli's living room on the parlor floor. Anita and Bertram Stomp owned the entire four-story brownstone on Henry Street. Our parents, including Liza's future stepfather, were in a loose cluster across the room, each with a pomegranate vodka cocktail in hand. My mom had already had two. With every drink, her voice went up a notch in volume. One more cocktail, and we'd have to distribute earplugs. Mom looked good—if stressed—tonight in her clingy Betsey Johnson party dress (she was pint-sized, like Joya). Dad stood next to her, grimly. Mom and Dad had had a whisper fight in their office when he finally got home, leaving him no time to bake a cake. He hated showing up empty-handed.

"This is supposed to be a Hicks Street reunion," said Liza. "Gary never lived on Hicks Street. My father should be here."

Eli, in bright red lipstick and a Morticia dress with a satin choker collar, looked like a Chinese vampire. "I haven't seen your dad in years," she said, slipping delicately on hot tea.

Neither had I. When I knew the man, Ryan had been a hedge fund manager on Wall Street. He wore a suit every day and carried a briefcase. Ryan wasn't a happy person, except when he took us to the Y to go swimming. All five of us. He'd lead us through the streets like a mother duck, and we were his obedient ducklings. Liza visited her dad in Bermuda a few times a year. I'd been waiting in vain for an invitation to join her. But she never shared her time with Ryan, not with me or anyone.

In an oversized sweatshirt and yoga pants, Liza looked like a teenage bag lady, clearly rebelling against Gary's presence by dressing out of her hamper.

I wore jeans and a royal blue cashmere turtleneck. Casual, but hot. (Standing by the fire, I was, in fact, roasting.) I wanted to transmit that I cared about my appearance but wasn't obsessed with it, which was how I imagined college girls operated. Matt would appreciate the effect, I hoped.

"Stanley should be here any minute," announced Liza suddenly.

Eli frowned. "I thought 'no boyfriends.'" Her mom's rule. Anita Stomp was a practical woman. The three families (counting Gary) totaled eleven people. Anita had service for twelve. Thinking about it, Eli added, "Stanley should add some color to the evening."

"As it were," I said. Marry, he would, and Liza knew that. Counted on it. "Does Stanley know you're sandbagging him?"

Liza shook her head. "I'm hoping he won't notice."

Eli and I laughed at that.

I glanced around the room, at the deep purple walls, the layers of Oriental carpet, the brass fixtures and mahogany screens. To go with the 1870 brownstone, Anita's decorating was meticulously, faithfully Victorian. Eli's dad, Bertram, was nearly a Victorian relic himself, pushing seventy years old. Anita was at least sixty, but dashed and darted around with the energy of a teenage ferret.

"That brings back memories," said Eli, pointing at one of the plum velour couches with lion's paw feet in the center of the room. "Joya and Matt, heads together over a coloring book."

Liza caught my eyes narrowing. "Jealous?" she asked.

"You don't object if Joya steals Matt's attention," I said.

"They're talking," said Liza. "Not grappling."

I blushed at the memory.

"Look at Dora," said Eli. "She's turning red."

Bong. Doorbell. Liza said, "He's here."

Anita Stomp excused herself from the adult conversation and answered the front door, which opened into the living room. She swung it open, and a cold wind blew through the room, making the fire jump and crackle.

"Hello?" asked Anita to Stanley in his parka.

"Stanley!" sang Liza, skipping over to him in her yoga pants. "I'm so glad you made it!" She threw her arms around him and pulled him down (way down) into a red-hot tongue kiss for the entire room of people to see.

To Eli I said, "One day we'll teach her about subtlety."

She said, "Stanley looks terrified."

It was an ancient terror, the blood memory of generations of black men who were hung or worse for kissing blond white women. He forcibly detached her and shook his head. Despite Liza's hopes, Stanley had sized up the situation in approximately two seconds.

He said, "You said seven o'clock."

The rest of us got here at six thirty. She'd staged his high-impact entrance like a prima grammarian. I'd known Liza my whole life. And this was, no question, the most selfish thing she'd ever done.

Anita held out her hand to her new guest. She said, "I'm Anita Stomp, the host. And you're Stanley, I presume. I thought I said 'no boyfriends.'" Anita was a balls-to-the-wall corporate lawyer who expected the rules to be followed. To the letter.

Liza said, "I'm so sorry! I forgot!"

Anita opened her mouth to call Liza on her big fat lie. I cringed, having been on the receiving end of Anita's summary judgments many times before. She relished the role of disciplinarian to her surrogate daughters. Liza braced for the attack, waited for it.

But she'd have to wait all night. Anita held her tongue (with her teeth) and invited Stanley inside. She took his coat, gave him a seltzer with lime and went to get another place setting from the kitchen.

Eli said, "I'd better explain to Mom," and made tracks for the kitchen. I suspected Anita had already figured out what was going on.

I walked over to Stanley, positioning my body between him and everyone else. I said softly, "Just stay by me, Stanley."

"I'm so angry right now," he whispered through clenched teeth. "She's using me again."

"She'll pay for it," I said. "But later." He nodded, our eyes locked, both of us pissed off at Liza's selfishness but understanding it, too. "I will not leave your side," I promised. "I'll be your human shield."

"Thanks, Dora," he said, smiling nervously. "Let's get the worst part over with."

My hand on his back, we walked to where Liza stood next to her mother and Gary. Myopic in her spite, Liza couldn't see Stanley's discomfort.

Stephanie held out her hand. "Hello, Stanley. Good to see you again." She smiled warmly at him, but stress was crinkling around her eyes.

He said, "I'm sorry I'm late," and shook Stephanie's hand. "Good evening, Mr. Glitch."

Stanley held out his hand.

Gary nodded at him gruffly. And didn't shake Stanley's hand. We watched it hanging out there for a beat of five. Liza upped the tension by slipping her arm around Stanley's waist. Gary bristled. He played with ice cubes in his cocktail, coughed uncomfortably. He said, "You're standing too close, young man. Please step back."

How could Stephanie marry this man?

Mom instantly picked up the vibes, too. Loud enough to alert the media *in Europe*, Mom yelled, "Stanley Nable! I haven't seen you since you were five feet tall! It's been, how long? A foot and a half? How's your mother?"

He said, "She's well."

In Gary's direction, Mom said, "Stanley's mother is the head of orthopedic surgery at LICH. And his father is a news editor for ESPN. Come over to the couch, Stanley. I want to hear all about what you've been up to."

I loved Mom at that second. Drunk and earsplitting, she was doing what she could to help. Keeping my promise, I stayed at Stanley's side. The three of us took over the couch facing Matt and Joya.

Mom and Stanley chatted. I listened with half an ear while I watched Liza and Stephanie hiss at each other in the corner. The three men—Dad, Gary and Bertram Stomp—tried to make small talk.

My gaze eventually wandered to the opposite couch. Joya was pointing at her sketchbook, explaining her technique (or whatever she prattled on about). Matt, meanwhile, was staring at me.

When our eyes connected, the surface temperature of my skin shot up twenty degrees. I had to look away—or spontaneously combust. When I dared to peek again (two seconds later), Matt Greene, the sun god, was still locked on me. But now he was grinning.

I won't torture you with the blow-by-blow, but suffice it to say that meal was the longest, tensest forty minutes of eating I've ever sat through. Stanley was furious at Liza. Liza was "ya see? ya see?"-ing all night about the way Gary treated Stanley (ignored and/or insulted). Mom felt compelled to change the subject of conversation—even when there was no conversation—and had to bring up (with shattering volume) the fact that Dad had spent most of the day looking for some sitar-strumming metallurgist ex-friend who'd stiffed them for five grand a million years ago. Joya sat next to Matt and peppered him with questions as heavily as she salted her spinach. He barely had a chance to shoot a secret smile at me. Eli seemed bemused by the spectacle. Her parents? Bewildered. Stephanie Greene? BOTHERED. She squirmed in her chair and stabbed at her beef.

At dessert, she finally came out with what she'd been waiting to get off her chest all night long.

"I'm pregnant," she said.

KIDDING! Stephanie Greene was fifty years old. Beyond pregnancy potential. But imagine how shocking that would have been! Liza would have spontaneously barfed in her hands.

(Look, this dinner was *tense*! I had to amuse myself somehow.)

What she really said: "Gary and I have been looking at houses in Westchester."

He said, "More than looking, Steph." To the table, Gary said, "We made an offer on a Tudor in Ossining."

Liza dropped her fork. Then she threw her spoon across the room like a petulant five-year-old. I couldn't say I blamed her.

"Whose idea was this?" she demanded of her mother.

Gary cleared his throat and took control. "It was my idea, and your mother agrees. I've always wanted to move to the suburbs and have more space. It's a beautiful house, Liza. A lot more space. A yard to play in."

"What, am I five years old?" asked Liza. "I didn't care about a *yard*. I'm going to college in two years. Less than that. You can't wait until I finish high school?"

"The house is half a mile from one of the best high schools in the state," said Stephanie. She took Gary's hand. "We want our life together to start as soon as possible. Since we both rent now, we can move in a matter of weeks."

"And take me out of Brownstone?" gasped Liza, approaching hysterics. "In the middle of the school year?"

Stephanie glanced nervously around the table. "Tuition is very expensive," she said.

Marry, if they pulled Liza out midyear, they'd save thousands of dollars.

"This isn't about money!" Liza said. "You refused to leave Brooklyn when Dad wanted to. He would've compromised on the burbs."

Good rebuttal. Stephanie Greene flapped her lips, and her eyes flitted around the table, searching for support, finally coming to rest on the sympathetic face of my mother.

Who again tried to change the subject. "Did any of you know the receivers of the bad check have to pay the fine on it?" she asked.

Bertram Stomp said, "I did not know that. In all my years of depositing checks, I don't think anyone's ever written me a bad one. What about you, Anita?"

With classic matter-of-fact delivery, Anita said, "It would be disruptive for Liza to switch schools in the middle of the year. And this is a crucial time for her. She's taking the SATs soon. Moving could shift her class ranking. And that could harm her chances at certain colleges."

Stephanie said, "I know, but Liza will manage. We're a family and we have to stick together. And this move is what Gary and I think is best for us. I'll miss Brooklyn—all of you—so much . . ."

Open the floodgates. Stephanie and Liza were both crying in their crème brûlée. Gary sat stone-faced, probably wondering what the hell he'd gotten himself into. "Come on, girls!" I hated that he called Stephanie a "girl." He added, "We're not moving to Siberia!"

"You might as well," I blurted.

Mom screamed, "Dora!"

Stanley's chair scraped as he pushed away from the table. The tension of the dinner had taken its toll on him. "No one in their right mind would leave Brooklyn, unless he was trying to get away from something in particular. Or someone," he said. "Thank you for an excellent meal, Mrs. Stomp." He went to Liza's chair and lifted her by the shoulders into a tight squeeze.

He kissed her on each cheek and said, "Good-bye." We all heard the finality of it. A real good-bye. Stanley hated being a pawn, and he knew when to admit defeat. Their relationship couldn't possibly survive with this much family disapproval. He glanced dolefully at me, grabbed his coat and left.

Naturally, I will never forgive him for leaving like that. If he'd had any sense of decency, he would have taken me with him.

Matt Greene stood, too, and comforted his mother and sister. He glared at Gary and wondered, as we all did, what his hold over Stephanie was that she would uproot their lives for him.

Gary had to be pretty good in bed, I theorized. But then again, any animal could screw.

The party couldn't limp on another minute after that horrible scene. Liza and Stephanie were still arguing as they exited the building. I could hear Liza's accusatory, "You, you, you" halfway down the block. Matt kissed and hugged all the mothers, slapped the backs of the fathers. He pecked Joya on the cheek, bussed Eli chastely on her knuckle. Matt approached me last (a good sign). He kissed me lightly on the cheek, half on the lips, and said, "I came here tonight to see you."

"And we didn't talk at all."

"We'll get our chance," he said, pressing a neatly folded note into my hand.

Without looking back, he ran to catch up with his splintered family. As soon as they were gone, Anita Stomp brought out the heavy shit—a big bottle of brandy. While the adults quaffed and bitched about the horrible influence of Gary on

Stephanie and the ramifications for poor Liza, the remaining offspring sulked on the couch. Eli was too shell-shocked to speak. She and Liza—one skinny and dark, the other curvy and fair—were best friends. Closer to each other than I was to either of them. I'd always known it. Eli, by nature an intellectual, a loner, tolerated few friends. I was sure she was imagining how lonely she'd be without Liza, even if she had me.

Joya, empathetic, was depressed on Eli's behalf. She actually started crying a little and turned to hug . . . *me*.

"We have each other," she whispered in my ear.

Then, before I could hug back or comment, Joya let me go and showered her attention on Eli.

I quietly unfolded the square of paper Matt had pressed into my palm. And read it.

Dora:

Meet me at the corner of W. 81st and CPW tomorrow (Sunday) at high noon. There's something big and round I want to show you.

P.S. Don't tell anyone.

Signed,

Your Not-So-Secret Admirer

Sixteen

Matt was standing on the corner of Eighty-first and Central Park West right on time, at noon. I was a few minutes late. It took some finagling to get out of the house. I told my parents I was going to the movies, alone, to process the devastation of the night before.

Joya dropped her square of toast and begged, "Can I come?"

"No way," I said.

"Sure you're not meeting someone?" she asked, making me wonder, not for the first time, if she had special powers.

Dad, as wrung out as a dishrag, said, "Alone means alone, Joya. If Dora wants privacy, she's entitled. However, should my darling firstborn prefer a benevolent nonjudgmental presence at her side—me, for example—I could clear my schedule."

"You're not going anywhere," said Mom acidly.

He frowned at his wife of twenty years, a woman he'd come to know as well as he knew himself. And one of the many finer points he'd picked up along the way was this: She didn't hangover gracefully.

"Dora," he implored, "help me."

"Sorry, Dad. You're on your own."

"I'm begging you!" he bellowed, and Mom swatted him on the head with the rolled-up *Times* Book Review.

It was sweet, this breakfast scene of domestic disquietude and unrest. But I had a rendezvous with a not-so-secret admirer, and I really had to fly.

"That's the biggest ball I've ever seen," I said, as Matt escorted me into the Rose Center for Earth and Space, aka the Planetarium at the Museum of Natural History on the lip of Central Park, on the Upper West Side of Manhattan. The planetarium was a four-story glass and steel cube with a three-story sphere inside. A ball in a box. The sphere was home to the planetarium's theater. Movies about space and stars were projected on the domed ceiling, giving true meaning to the phrase "theater in the round." I'd been here on school field trips and been duly wowed.

"Check this out," said Matt, leading me into the lobby, flashing his staff pass, getting approving nods from security. "Step on this scale," he said. "Your weight on the surface of the Sun: 3,110 pounds. You might want to cut down on the Twinkies, Dora."

"I've never had a Twinkie in my life, you jerk," I said, punching him in the arm.

He stepped on the scale. His weight on the Sun: 3,543 pounds. "We're heavier on the Sun because of its gravitational density," he said.

I gazed at his radiant smile, his halo of blond hair. "Gravity," I said, feeling it pull me closer to him.

I checked my weight on the nine planets and the Moon (where I weighed practically nothing). "I've got a get-rich-quick idea," I said to Matt as we walked (holding hands) to the second floor of the Gottesman Hall of Planet Earth.

"Go on," he said.

"The Scales of Venus," I said. My weight on Venus was only 108 pounds. "It'll show your reduced weight, reflecting that lighter-than-air feeling of being in love."

"Is that how it works? Fall in love, walk on air?" he asked.

I cleared my throat and talked like a professor. "When infatuated, the brain releases certain chemicals that act as natural appetite suppressants. Dopamine and norepinephrine, for example. So one does, actually, lose weight at the beginning of a new relationship."

"I'm impressed," he said. "You learned this at Brownstone?"

"*Self* magazine," I said. "Don't laugh! Women's magazines are about more than dresses and lipsticks."

"I was surprised to see Noel Kepner at your place last week," he said abruptly. "I thought you were over."

"We are now," I said. "Liza and I had a fight about you."

He paused. "We talked about you, too. But she can't be taken seriously lately."

"With good reason!"

"There's *always* a good reason," he said. "My sister is an emotionally needy person. The fact that she's always in crisis doesn't mean the world revolves around her." We walked by a scale model of the planets revolving around the Sun.

"Your mom is marrying a cretin racist. That isn't exactly a broken fingernail," I said, defending Liza.

"That's Mom's problem," he said succinctly.

My subconscious should have waved some warning flags about Matt then. But it didn't, and I shrugged off his comments. He was an older brother, and he probably didn't get as much attention from his parents after the beautiful baby Liza was born. His resentment ran deep. I could relate. I'd been jealous of Joya since my parents brought her home from the hospital.

Matt said, "This way to the Heilbrunn Cosmic Pathway." He tugged me toward a spiraling ramp that circled the giant sphere.

He explained as we walked: "The Big Bang occurred thirteen billion years ago. If the length of this ramp represents all time, from the Big Bang until the present day—each foot representing ten million years—humans have existed on Earth for the equivalent of the width of a single hair."

I droned, "We are tiny cosmic blips. Our lives are insignificant. All existence is meaningless."

Matt laughed and said, "Nine out of ten people who walk this exhibit say the same thing."

"So what's the point, Star Man?" I asked. "Why are we here? On Earth?"

"You're asking me?" he said, grinning. "You *are*? Okay. Big question. Bigger minds than mine have failed to answer it. From an anthropological standpoint, I'd say we are here to eat, mate and survive. From an astronomical standpoint, I'd say we're just lucky accidents. The Earth is what's important, our planet's place in the solar system. We're here to keep the Earth spinning."

"Interesting," I said. "Want my take on this situation?"

"Do I," he said, a glint like a star in his eyes. We were winding our way uphill, toward the dawning of time.

"You're taking a semester off from college," I said. "To meet Gary, be part of the wedding, do this sweet internship. Hanging out at Stephanie's place sucks. Your job maybe isn't all you expected. None of your friends from Brownstone are around. You said you've always liked me. So I'm your convenient, available amusement. For my part, I never liked you before. But I do now. And, as you said, the best way to get over one guy is to hook up with another."

Matt said, "I thought you were going to explain the meaning of life."

"I am," I said. "My life."

Matt nodded. "I noticed how you treated Stanley last night. Took care of him," he said, guiding me toward a side door by the theater entrance with a sign that read, EMPLOYEES ONLY.

"Just doing my job," I said.

"You like to operate behind the scenes," he said. "You're a nudge in the right direction. You give the little pushes. Right?"

I nodded slightly, vainly.

Matt said, "And I bet your friends don't always thank you for what you do."

We'd entered a dark, empty space.

"Where are we?" I asked.

Matt said, "This is the space show theater. It's being renovated during the winter. Construction guys work around the clock, Monday through Saturday."

It was Sunday. We took seats in the quiet room. The dark movie screen on the rounded ceiling was covered in white paint speckles that looked like stars in the night sky.

I said, "It's freezing in here."

He instantly put his arm around me. We sat in silence, looking at the starry ceiling. Then he said, "I don't get lighter-than-air feelings when I'm in love. The world stays solidly under my feet. Relationships are grounding. If I meet someone I want to spend time with, I do. We have so little time, relatively speaking, on Earth to waste."

"Relationships are deeper than that," I said. "They're tests of trust and commitment and sacrifice."

"That doesn't sound like much fun," he said. "Did you read that in *His-and-Her Dating*?"

I grumbled, "No." But I had.

"I like spending time with you," he declared. "We can fool around. Up to you."

Was it really that easy? I like you, let's snog? How great life would be if everyone would be so direct. "You make a convincing argument," I admitted.

He laughed. I liked the sound of it, how his neck muscles stretched. Even though I knew exactly who he was and where he came from, Matt seemed like an alien creature to me. From Planet Do-Me.

I kissed him. I pushed up the armrest between our chairs and planted a wet one on his pink lips. I didn't ask first. I violated the Brownstone code of conduct. I broke my promise to Liza. I betrayed my lingering attachment to Noel. But at that moment (in time, so precious, shouldn't waste it), I didn't care about anyone or anything but Matt and that mouth.

And he tasted so good. I was inflamed by his kiss and went at it with more passion and aggression than ever. He was all over me, too. His hand went under my shirt, tugged it out of my pants, and I shivered. I dug under his clothes. He moaned when my fingers touched his taut, hairless chest.

I thought, Mission: Matt. To seek uncharted experiences, to boldly go where I had never been before.

And then the theater door opened. A wedge of light spilled into the dark room. We broke apart and turned toward the intruder—another researcher?—who saw us and babbled an apology before leaving.

Matt said, "We should go." He looked worried, like he might get in trouble for bringing someone in here.

We stood up. My legs were wobbly. I said, "Well, I saw stars."

He smiled and took me back down the Cosmic Pathway. We were quiet as we walked forward in time, ten million years per step.

"You never told me," he said, "what you want to do after high school."

"I want to be a writer," I said. "So predictable, right? Because of my parents. Embarrassing, really. I haven't told anyone else."

He said, "I'm glad you chose me."

Seventeen

Upon my return home, I gave my family a scathing critique of the movie I hadn't seen (but had read a few reviews of). I responded to an e-mail from Liza, assuring her that Matt, who'd made himself scarce all day, wasn't abandoning her but was dealing with their family issues in his own way, like most men, in solitude.

All that lying ruined my good night's sleep. I tossed and turned, replaying the kiss with Matt, his soft hair against my cheek, how my heart nearly hatched when he got his hand under my shirt. As I flipped around on my bed, I twisted mentally, too, fully aware of my own contradictory impulses. Doing something bad felt good *because it was bad*. Would I have been as excited if Matt weren't a secret?

By dawn, I'd done enough self-analysis to last the rest of

my life. I threw back the covers, froze, turned blue, and dove back into bed. I counted to fifty, summoned bravery, and then got up, washed, dressed, wrote a note to Mom to explain my absence at breakfast and went to Brownstone.

I got there at seven in the morning. I kept my head down as I walked, not wanting to be noticed (although, with my sherpa hat, parka and scarf, Sherlock Holmes wouldn't have been able to pick me out of a lineup). I climbed the steps of the school and pulled on the door handle.

Locked. Shit.

I pushed the security buzzer. No one answered. I leaned on it for thirty seconds. No response.

Double shit.

I started banging on the door, yelling to be let in. So much for stealth. After a few freezing minutes, the door opened. Mr. Contralto, the school custodian, stood on the inside, irritated and confused. "Ms. Benet? Classes are not for an hour."

"Bright and early Monday morn," I sang. "I can't *wait* to learn, Mr. Contralto."

"Learn what?" he asked, like he knew something.

He let me inside, and I started to regain feeling in my toes. "The truth is"—a good windup for *another* lie—"I left my books in my locker and I came as soon as I could to do my homework."

Mr. Contralto, an honest, hardworking man who, I'd always suspected, resented the entitlement of some of Brownstone's students (not me, of course), said, "I can't let you loose in the school unsupervised."

"I'll just get my books and do my homework in the cafeteria."

He nodded, suspicious. He checked his watch; he had things to do. "Okay."

I jogged down the hallway to the upper school locker area, sure he was watching me. After gathering some books, I went straight for Chez Brownstone. Some cafeteria workers were already there, preparing what would be our lunch. I spread out my books and backpack on one of the long tables and waited. Sure enough, Mr. Contralto walked through ten minutes later, ostensibly to inspect the room, but I knew he was checking on me. I waved at him with both hands, and said, "Thanks ever so, Mr. Contralto."

He barely acknowledged me and walked off, his key chain jangling on his belt.

I stood up, stretched, and then too obviously grabbed my lower belly. Anyone watching would've assumed I'd been stricken with a sudden, uncontrollable urge to urinate. I hobbled down the aisle of the cafeteria, but instead of veering to the right toward the girls' room, I went left and tiptoed up the stairway toward the teachers' lounge, aka Ms. Matilda Rossi's office.

The door was miraculously (thanks, God) unlocked. I opened it, cringing when it creaked, and slipped inside. I considered locking the door behind me, but decided against it.

I went right for her desk—also unlocked. Marry, why would she bother? The drawers and hanging folders were completely empty. I did find a stack of papers in her in-box.

Graded essays we'd turned in last week on Shakespeare's use of symbolism in *Romeo and Juliet*. Riffling through them, I saw that she'd give A's to all the boys (even Freddy Pluto, whose paper had five typos in the first line). She'd given Bs or Cs to the girls. Including me, writing in red ink that the "light and dark symbols are old news." Of course they were old! The play itself was five hundred years old!

So Ms. Rossi was not a girl's girl. Knew it already. I wondered what torture she'd endured at my age to turn her against her own gender. Had there been a Sondra Fortune in Rossi's past? No, I realized. Matilda Rossi would have *been* the Sondra Fortune in her high school. She'd developed a taste for cruelty that hadn't diminished with age. That epiphany, more than the fear of getting caught searching a teacher's desk, hit me like a hurricane.

And then, the creaking sound of the door. It was opening! A lesser girl would have frozen in her booties, or screamed in terror. Not I! Holding my shit together, I crawled into the tiny cranny between a radiator and a bookshelf. Even in my acute anxiety, I was impressed that I was small enough to fit into such a skinny space.

Clacking on the wood floor confirmed my worst fears. Ms. Rossi, in slutty stiletto heels, had entered the room. I heard the scraping of her metal chair as she pulled it back to sit. The aroma of gray Chez Brownstone coffee wafted into my nostrils, mixing nauseatingly with her peony perfume. She picked up her desk phone and pushed buttons.

"You there?" she asked. "Five minutes. And don't let anyone see you." Ms. Rossi hung up. I listened to her blow on her coffee and turn the pages of a newspaper. In a cannonball position, my legs started to cramp. But if I stretched an inch, I'd be discovered.

The door creaked again. A cheerful (for a Monday morning) male voice—one I knew only too well—said, "Good morning. You look great today."

"Thank you," she said, lapping up the flattery like a kitten lapped cream.

"You're incredible," he gushed. "I can't believe you even talk to me."

She practically purred and said, "Have you done what I asked?"

He paused and then confessed, "I had a busy weekend. My parents dragged me to my grandparents' house, and I had to help them put new contact paper on their kitchen shelves."

"That's no excuse," she spit, her claws out, finally.

"I'm sorry! I'll do it later today!"

"Do it now," she said.

"I have class in ten minutes," he stammered.

"Then you'd better hurry," she commanded.

The squeak and shuffle of sneakers running for the door, followed by the creak of the door closing. Ms. Rossi drank her coffee, read the newspaper. At two minutes of eight, she clacked out of the room, closing the door behind her.

My legs were, by now, asleep. Pins and needles savaged my muscles as blood rushed back into the limbs. I stood up and hobbled out of the lounge and down the stairs.

Chez Brownstone was now full of lower school kids

eating breakfast, waiting for their teachers to collect them for the start of their classes at eight thirty. My belongings had been pushed to the end of the long table, my backpack half spilled on the floor. I gathered my stuff and limp-ran to class. Ms. Rossi's class. I'd be late, and she'd skewer me like a kabob for it.

As I neared my destination, my heart pulsing the Morse code for ARGH!, I tried to make sense of what I'd heard. Sondra would want to know every detail. That was what she (wasn't) paying me for. And there was someone else who'd need a complete report, too. I would try to avoid that conversation for as long as possible.

Which was approximately five seconds. Three doors away from my English lit classroom, I nearly crashed into Eli Stomp, herself running late to advanced biology.

She said, "Dora! Are you okay? You look weird."

"Just late, and soon to be strung up by the ovaries," I said. Daring to meet her eyes, I said, "You look a bit freaky yourself."

"Eric was supposed to meet me at Grind for breakfast and he never showed," she said. "I waited as long as I could. Where the hell *is* he?"

I gave her a look of utter bafflement, way overdoing it. She asked, "Have you seen him?"

"Absolutely *not*," I said truthfully. I hadn't *seen* him. But I had heard him—in Matilda Rossi's office, kissing her princess ass, making her promises, declaring his devotion.

"Lunch at Chez?" she called as she dashed off.

"You betcha," I said.

Eighteen

"You're late!" snipped Ms. Rossi.

"And I'm sorry!" I said, trying to sound genuine. "I have no good excuse, and you'll probably want to berate me in front of all these witnesses. I mean, *people*. In front of all these people."

She hissed, "Sit."

I sat. I would have gladly rolled over and played dead if she wanted. Liza, seated next to me, shot me a glance of sympathy, undercurrent of amusement, overtones of desperation. She could do five emotions in three seconds and still save a few for later. Stanley, seated a few rows behind, made an intensive study of the top of his desk. Noel seemed to be looking right at me. But then I realized he was actually looking right through me, as if I weren't there.

Wished I weren't.

Ms. Rossi said, "*Romeo and Juliet*, by the middle of act two, is really heating up. The characters are sneaking around, lying to their families, getting others to do their dirty work. They're taking huge risks, and not thinking about the potentially explosive consequences of their actions."

I swallowed hard. Life—mine—was imitating art a mite too closely for comfort.

"Dora and Noel," said Ms. Rossi, "we're at your scene. Let me set the stage. Juliet has sent Nurse to arrange an assignation with Romeo. Nurse, an overprotective shrew, reluctantly agrees to do Juliet's bidding. Romeo, for his part, is annoyed he has to deal with this old hag when all he really wants is to spend time with his beautiful Juliet."

"We get the picture," I said. And then slapped a hand over my mouth while Rossi glared at me.

Noel said, "Can we just get on with it?"

Ms. Rossi said, "Let's. Freddy as Mercutio. You're in this scene, too. Pray, start at the top of page sixty."

Freddy said, " 'The bawdy hand of the dial is now on the prick of noon.' " Then he added, "I said 'prick.' "

" 'What a man you are,' " I said. What a moron he was, marry.

Noel read his lines in a drone, not the lovesick puppy he was supposed to be.

I liked this scene. I got to say "troth," "scurvy knave," "flirt-gills," "skains-mates," and "I'm so vexed that every part of me quivers." Romeo's lines were blabbering verbosity, so it wasn't a stretch for Noel. Freddy got to recite a quatrain about a "hare hoar" (which he pronounced "hairy whore") who was "too much for a score."

Shakespeare was a perv.

I got emotional, reading lines with Noel, the boy who'd told me he loved me, made me believe it, and then tossed me aside like a sack of garbage. That was to say, I was getting angry all over again. When I delivered Nurse's famous line to Romeo, warning him not to lead Juliet into a "fool's paradise," which would constitute "gross behavior" and was an "ill thing" that was "very weak dealing," I spit it out, laid the distrust on thick. I shot him dagger glances, too.

Noel recoiled at my vehemence. He seemed to be speaking to me (Dora) when he said, " 'I doth protest.' "

"You doth?" I asked.

"That's not your line, Nurse," said Ms. Rossi.

Noel raised his hand. "May I speak on Romeo's behalf?"

"We're not finished with the scene."

Noel went on nevertheless, "Nurse seems to think that Romeo is this untrustworthy jerk who intends to ruin Juliet's life. It's true, Romeo did have a reputation for going from girl to girl. I can see how, if Juliet or Nurse knew about his past, they might worry about it. But Romeo's feelings for Juliet are different than for those other girls. He might get pissed off at her, but he would never have betrayed her."

I said, "But he suddenly stopped contacting her. He dropped off the face of the earth."

"No, Nurse," said Ms. Rossi. "That doesn't happen until later in the play. Act three."

Noel said, "Romeo had no choice! He had to back away and think about what was happening. It had to be a real separation or he wouldn't have been able to figure out what he wanted."

I said, "For all his thoughtfulness, Romeo is a physical, sexual person. And Juliet is clearly more reserved."

"Not so," said Noel. "Juliet is aggressive. She kissed him after three minutes, made plans to hook up with him after one conversation. Maybe Juliet is using Romeo to get sexual experience. Since she has none."

I gasped. Anyone with half a neuron knew we'd really been talking about our own relationship. Noel might as well have stood up on his desk, pointed at me and screamed, "Virgin!" Half the class was giggling. Even Ms. Rossi chuckled (blast her eyes!). I might have thrown up in my mouth, but I can't say for sure because I died of embarrassment.

Nineteen

"I don't get why you're freaking out," said Liza later at lunch. "It's not like your mother is marrying a Klansman."

Eli added, "You're not going to die a virgin."

"I already did," I corrected her. "Of embarrassment."

Liza took a bite out of her Chez Brownstone turkey wrap sandwich. While chewing, she said, "It was one moment of your life, Dora. Get over it."

"But life is one moment after the next," I philosophized. "Each moment is a direct result of what came before. It determines what comes next. Each moment is like a year, or a decade, or a millennium. It's a fragment of the future. But, actually, you're right. None of it matters. The Earth will collide with the Sun in a million years. We're just insignificant specks. Our existence is meaningless."

Eli said, "So now you're a nihilist. A virgin nihilist."

Liza said, "You sound like Matt." And then her blue eyes widened as big as the ocean. "I asked you to stay away from him."

"I haven't seen your brother," I lied. "And, frankly, Liza, it might not be such a bad thing if I did. He might be in need of emotional support, too. And he's certainly not getting it from you."

We were distracted when Sondra Fortune and Lori Dropov swept into the cafeteria like they owned it, which, for all intents and purposes, they did.

Sondra stopped at our table. "Fringe," she said. "How's it going?"

"You honor me with your acknowledgment," I said.

"It's been so long since we had a chat," said Sondra. "We should catch up." Her way of asking me if I had any news to report.

Over her shoulder, Lori Dropov made a fist and smacked it into her open palm. "No need," I said. "I have absolutely nothing interesting to say." My way of telling her I was still gathering information.

"How sad for you," Sondra sniffed and then slinked off, Lori Dropov pulled along in her wake.

Eli squinted at me. She knew something was up, but, thankfully, she decided to ignore it.

Liza leaned forward and said, "I heard from Kim Daniels that Sondra and Vin Transom had a big fight this morning. Or, rather, Sondra was going off on him, and he just stood there, silent as a stone. And then, as Kim put it, 'Vin told her to LEAVE HIM ALONE, and walked away while Sondra was STILL YELLING AT HIM.'"

We laughed at Liza's impersonation of Kim Daniels, Teeming Masses loudmouth. But privately I felt Sondra's pain. She wasn't used to being treated like that, especially not by her previous stable of slavishly compliant boyfriends. She would take out her frustration on those closest to her, meaning Lori and Micha. And their frustration would trickle down the social food chain. To me.

Eli said, "The winter trimester is only three weeks old and nearly every fall-semester couple has already broken up. Except for me and Eric."

I opened my mouth and then shut it. Unlike Kim Daniels, I wasn't going to blab, at least not until I had proof. I stood up.

"Leaving so soon?" asked Eli.

"I'm off to lose my virginity," I said. "I'm open to all comers. As it were."

"Come one, come all," said Eli.

"Seriously, I have a meeting with Ratzenberger," I said. "We're going to discuss my *future*."

Eli and Liza both cringed at the idea of being alone in a room with the officious head of the upper school. I'd set up the meeting myself that morning between classes, ostensibly to talk about an appropriate direction for my unformed aspirations. But I had a secret agenda.

"Tell me what you want to be when you grow up," said the old woman, herself in her seventies.

"I am grown-up," I said.

"When you get out of high school," said Ms. Ratzenberger.

"That's the rub," I said, trying to sound adolescently confused. "I just don't *know*. I've been looking around for role models. I have to say, Ms. Ratzenberger, I'd be lucky to be like you."

"Ms. Benet! I'm flattered!" she said and smiled brightly, which took hours off her face.

"You, and Ms. Rossi," I said. "She seems like a super-nice person."

"She is a very accomplished young woman," agreed Ms. Ratzenberger. "And so attractive."

"I already know about *your* esteemed background," I said. Marry, everyone knew the upper school director's life story, since she reminded the students, parents and staff of her degrees, awards and years of Brownstone service in every newsletter, speech and annual report she issued. I continued, "But I don't know nearly enough about Ms. Rossi. What schools did she go to, for instance. Where else has she taught?"

"I'll have to tell Matilda that she's got an ardent fan," said Ms. Ratzenberger.

"NO!" I shouted. "I'll be way too embarrassed."

"I understand," she said and winked her wrinkled eyelid. I felt a pang of guilt, deceiving this earnest woman who, despite her years of working with teenagers, continued to think the best of everyone, including me. Poor deluded woman.

She reached into a cabinet behind her, searching for the

Rossi papers. "I have her file right here," she said, laying it wide open on her desk.

"Please tell me everything," I said. "I can't wait!"

That might have been pushing it. Ms. Ratzenberger looked over her glasses at me, suspicious. I smiled angelically.

"Matilda Rossi comes to us from Saint Paul's School in New Hampshire," she said, dragging her knotty index finger along the pages. "Before that, she was an assistant teacher at Phillips Exeter Academy, also in the Granite State. She left there for . . . it says 'personal reasons.' She graduated from the University of Massachusetts and continued there to earn her master's in English literature. She completed her master's in teaching at the University of New Hampshire while teaching at Exeter."

"Wow!" I said. "Plus, she did all that modeling for J.Crew."

"Yes," said Ms. Ratzenberger, her brow a cable knit of concern. "We've all seen that in the *Brief*."

" 'Brief' is the word," I said. "The skirt, I mean."

"For the record, Ms. Benet," she said sternly, "I have spoken to Ms. Rossi about her contributions to the student newspaper. And she sees the wisdom of discretion and modesty."

So Rossi had been scolded by the boss. I was encouraged. "I think it's really sweet, how Ms. Rossi holds office hours all day long in the teachers' lounge," I said. "There's always a long line of boys—*students*—to speak with her. And it's a testament to her teaching abilities that most of the boys—*students*—aren't taking any of her classes! She's inspiring to the boys—I mean, the students. Igniting that spark of intellectual curiosity."

Ms. Ratzenberger said, "Quite."

"I'd better go to class now," I said.

"One minute," said Ms. Ratzenberger. "I want to discuss something with you. Privately. A matter of sensitivity."

That made me freeze. "What?"

"How are things at home lately?"

What the . . . ? "Fine," I said. "Great."

"I'm glad to hear it."

"And you are asking because?"

"I just want you to know that if there is anything wrong, you can come to me, or Joya can go to Ms. Templeton." Templeton was head of the middle school.

"Is this about Joya?"

"I'm only reminding you that resources are available to both you and your sister."

"Look, Joya's overly sensitive. If our parents have a totally normal, everyday fight, she freaks out. I can only imagine the depths of her depression if they ever got divorced."

Ms. Ratzenberger asked softly, "Are your parents fighting often?"

"No!"

"Good."

"We're a blissfully close, happy family," I said. "We make other families look like the Simpsons."

She paused, frowned. "The O. J. Simpsons?"

A wall of steely defensiveness materialized between us.

Ratzenberger was clearly fishing for info about Joya. If anything was bothering my sister, it was none of her business. I would fix it. Joya was my sister to protect. No one else had any right to interfere with her. I looked at the well-intended, wizened face of Ms. Ratzenberger, and I perceived a clear threat.

"Joya is fine," I repeated and left.

Twenty

Joya wasn't home after school. Neither were my parents. I had no idea where everyone was, and I was starting to wonder if they were purposely having conferences to discuss the family's problems without me. The apartment felt empty and the sound of silence was unnerving. I'd long resented my parents' omnipresence at home—always so *here*, drinking coffee, hunched over the keyboard together or asking me intrusive questions—but now I missed them. Not that I'd talk to them if they were home. But the silence felt like an insult.

I called Matt Greene on his cell.

He said, "You should be glad your parents aren't dragging you into Joya's crisis. Do you honestly want to devote your energy to someone else's problem?"

"I feel left out," I whined. "Alone."

He said, "One second, Dora." He was at the planetarium, and from the sound of muffled voices, I gathered he was talking to a boss. He came back on. "I've got two minutes."

"So make with the advice," I said, stunned that I'd ask for it, since I'd spent so much time avoiding it.

"There are six and half billion people on this planet," said Matt. "You're not alone. If anything, as a species, we're *too* not alone."

"I'm a person," I said. "Not a species."

"If you want to feel crowded, move to India," he said. "Otherwise, I'll take you to dinner."

"When?" I said. "I'm hungry now."

He laughed and said, "I like a woman with a healthy appetite. I'll be there in two hours."

Matt picked me up in one hour and forty-eight minutes. He called me from my stoop because the buzzer was broken. I left a note for my parents—who hadn't shown up, nor had Joya—to hire an electrician to fix it. Just another example of how all systems broke down when one of them was ignored.

And I was that ignored system.

I greeted Matt downstairs, wearing the equivalent of a down comforter on my back.

Matt said, "You look sexy in that coat."

"Please."

He said, "Seriously. It makes me think of going to bed."

"Let's go to dinner instead. You're paying, College Boy," I said, "so you get to pick the restaurant."

"I know just the place," he said.

He made me walk forever. At least five blocks. And then we ducked into the new Indian restaurant, So Suri, on Atlantic Avenue. "Since I said 'India' to you, I've been thinking of Samosas."

The decorating appealed to my lasting childlike fascination with shiny, sparkly things. The beaded tablecloths, the Christmas lights around the windows and along the ceiling. The gold plates and tasseled napkin holders. The couch seating was upholstered in jewel-toned red and purple velvet and covered with satin pillows. Matt directed me onto a cozy love seat and then sat next to me instead of in a chair across the table.

That was when I noticed we were the only customers in there.

An eager and obsequious waiter—white napkin draped on his forearm—came over to offer us menus. Matt waved them aside and ordered for us. Without asking me what I wanted. He had a tendency, I was realizing, to do whatever he wanted. This notion both annoyed and excited me. Much as I tried to get my opinions heard, there was a brainless relief in letting someone else make decisions for me.

I wondered if this meant I was destined to become a housewife in the burbs with a bunch of dirty, bratty kids to take care of.

That, I swore to myself, would never happen. If I had one ambition in life, it was to have ambition.

Matt ordered a Taj Mahal beer. He asked if I wanted one,

too, and I declined. It was a Monday night, for Christ's sake. I generally kept my underage drinking to the weekends.

I got a Diet Coke. Matt Greene watched me drink, the bottle of beer to his own lips. When I put my glass back down on the table, he started to kiss me along the neck. Then up to my ear, around to my lips. He was leaving no skin untouched. The slow, steady journey of his lips made me feel woozy, dizzy.

The waiter cleared his throat to serve our appetizers, including Matt's Samosas, little triangular pastries filled with spiced meat and potatoes, along with a daisy wheel of sauces and oval puffs of bread.

While we ate, I asked, "You really don't involve yourself in anyone else's problems? You're a hands-off kind of guy?"

He put his fork-free hand on my thigh. "Getting involved is unavoidable sometimes. But, yeah, I'd rather not have to deal with it. I understand that some people like it. Your parents have made a great career out of other people's problems. Not for me."

"You make it sound like my parents have capitalized on woe. They've made a career out of *helping* people."

Matt said, "No offense, Dora. I love your family. I love my family. I feel bad that Liza and Mom are at each other's throats."

"But you like to keep your distance," I said, thinking of the thousands of miles Ryan Greene had put between himself and his family.

"I'm a very meat-and-potatoes kind of guy," said Matt,

while eating his meat-and-potato pockets. "Simple. Easy to understand. No hidden meaning. No secret ingredients. No hidden agenda." His hand moved farther up my thigh.

"I'm more of a salad myself," I said.

He came in for a taste. His lips were slightly greasy from the Samosa, but he smelled of spice and butter and I licked his lips.

I should be like Matt. Put some emotional distance between myself and everyone else. Mom and Dad's bickering had nothing to do with me. Joya could trip down her "bumpy patch" by herself. Liza's trouble with her mom and Stanley, Eli's sneaky boyfriend, Sondra's jealousy, Lori's and Micha's paranoia. Noel Kepner's resentment. I would take a giant step back from all of them. Be unconcerned and uncaring. Their problems were no longer mine.

I broke the kiss with Matt and grabbed his last morsel of Samosa. "I want to try it," I said, sampling the simple life.

Twenty-one

A Brooklyn Winter's Tale
Week IV, Scene I
The Benets' kitchen, Tuesday before school

"I have an announcement," I said at the dining room table.

Mom, in her bathrobe, mug of coffee in hand, said, "No more announcements, please."

Apparently, other announcements had been made yesterday, while my family was out somewhere ignoring me, about which I wasn't in the loop.

Dad, in his bathrobe, said, "You're announcing your engagement to Noel?"

"*What?*" I shrieked. "No! Noel and I broke up. We are no more. He dumped me, cruelly and coldly, and I'm glad. Because if he hadn't shown me the true nature of love, I wouldn't have reached the stage of enlightenment I'm at now."

"Which is?" asked Dad, grinning obnoxiously.

"From this point on, I am an island."

"Any particular island?" asked Mom.

"I am a separate, isolated entity," I explained. "I don't want to be interfered with, and I won't interfere with anyone else."

Joya plopped her spoon in her Lucky Charms and said, "Me, too. I want everyone to leave me alone!"

Mom and Dad shot her a look, and I could only guess what had gone down yesterday afternoon. A meeting at school with the middle school director? What had been discussed or decided? Was Joya on probation? Had Mom and Dad punished her for slacking? Maybe even forbade her from seeing Ben Teare until she got her grades up?

Stop, I told myself. You are not involved.

I said, "And now, I'm taking my toast and leaving. I'd say, 'Have a nice day,' but I don't want to assert undue influence on you. Instead, I'll just say, 'Have a day.'"

Dad said, "Have a day, yourself."

Week IV, Scene II
The upper school locker hallway, Tuesday early afternoon

I was minding my own business, as was my new modus operandi, when Sondra Fortune, alone and unescorted by her entourage, approached me. In public. For all the world to see.

"Got anything yet?" she asked. Her green eyes (which

contrasted dramatically with her mocha latte skin) seemed to be pleading.

I shrugged and said, "I want you to understand, Sondra, that if I persist in this case, it's for my own personal satisfaction. Anything I come up with is confidential. I know you're eager for revenge." I paused, not sure if I should say (but did), "I heard you and Vin broke up."

Those green eyes flashed at me, changing from vulnerable and needy to enraged in a (literal) blink. "Who told you?"

"It's all over school," I said. Thanks to Kim Daniels and her BULLHORN OF A MOUTH.

"It would be," she said flatly. Sondra knew her peccadilloes were hot gossip. They always had been, by virtue of her position as queen of the Ruling Class. Usually, she liked being on everyone's lips and minds. However, I suspected Sondra would rather have kept this particular relationship's demise private.

I felt a crack in my resolve. She looked so sad. "Rossi may have lied to Ms. Ratzenberger about her teaching history. I have some calls out." I'd left messages at Exeter, St. Paul's and the University of Massachusetts to confirm dates. An island needed to keep herself occupied. I'd spent a few hours Googling and found a two-year hole in Rossi's résumé, for the years 2003 and 2004.

Sondra nodded, a glint of happiness struggling for life in her eyes. "I don't need to know the details. But promise me you'll keep digging."

"You know, Sondra—not that it's any of my concern, since I don't *do* concern—but it might be possible that Vin

Transom's interest in Ms. Rossi had nothing to do with your breakup."

Sondra smiled (shark) and said, "Were you in bed with us?"

"I don't believe so," I said. "I think I would have remembered if I—"

"Then you have no idea what went wrong," she said.

Week IV, Scene III
Chez Brownstone, Thursday lunch

"I'm disgusted. I might puke on my tray," said Eli, who was usually way too refined to mention puke, let alone do it.

A copy of the new *Brief* was spread out on our table, open to the two-page story written by Eric Brainard, calling for the Brownstone community to rally behind our president and support the war to spread democracy in the Middle East.

Liza said, "Did you have any idea he felt this way?"

Eli said, "No! His parents are huge Democratic fundraisers. We've talked about the war a million times, and he's always said he thought it was a mistake."

I said, "Well, he's showing his true colors now. Face it, Eli. Your boyfriend is red."

Brooklyn Heights, incidentally, was perhaps the bluest neighborhood in New York, which was the bluest city in the bluest state in the nation. We were so blue, we were practically green.

Eli shook her head in disbelief. "This makes me question everything he's ever said."

"As in, 'I love you' and 'I want you'?" I asked.

Liza said, "Maybe the editorial is ironic."

Eli and I blinked at Liza and her cockeyed optimism. Eli said, "He never mentioned a word of this to me, and he usually talks about what he's writing, obsessively."

I was thrilled, of course, by this turn of events. I would have encouraged Eli to exfoliate Eric from her life like dead skin, but that would mean I'd be getting involved.

"Is Jack Carp a Republican?" I asked.

"God, no. I don't think there's a musician alive, any creative person, who would dare—wait a minute. What are you implying, Dora? That I'm attracted to Republicans?"

"At least one," I said, pointing at the newspaper.

Liza said, "Don't worry, Eli. No one is going to assume you agree with Eric's editorial. Just because you're his girlfriend doesn't mean you share his views."

The thought hadn't occurred to Eli until then. Paranoid, she glanced around the cafeteria. Sure enough, a bunch of students were staring rudely in our direction.

Eli stood up and made a big show of crumpling the newspaper into a tight ball. She walked to the central garbage can to throw it away. Then she poured a cup of coffee in on top of it and emptied a bottle of ketchup from the condiment table on top of that. Then she kicked the garbage can. So much for Eli's inscrutability.

Her vehemence earned her a smattering of applause, Liza clapping the loudest.

Week IV, Scene IV
The hallway outside of English lit, Friday morning

"I can't take much more of this," said Liza as we exited Ms. Rossi's classroom. "Mom and Gary are taking me to see the house in Ossining tomorrow."

"Oh," I said, trying to sound disinterested. Of all the people in my life, Liza was the most persistent in trying to involve me in her problems.

"Matt refuses to come. He says he's not going to live there, so he doesn't need to see it," she whined.

That I knew already. Matt had called me last night to tell me he'd have the run of his apartment all day, and he asked me to come over to "enjoy spending time together."

Yes, I'd been given a similar invitation from Noel when his parents were going out, and I turned him down. But that was a long time ago (four weeks). I had a different mind-set now. Noel had invited me over for sex. Matt just wanted to spend time with me. I knew the distinction in my head was only semantics (I was not now, nor had I ever been, an idiot). Both boys wanted the same thing. With Noel, sex would have been heavy. It would have carried emotional weight. Matt was a scientist at keeping it light. I told him I'd be there.

I said to Liza, "So you sit in the car, you look at the house, you drive home." Oozing ennui.

"Come with us," she said.

God. "I can't."

"Why not?"

"Plans," I said.

"What plans?"

"I'm . . . taking care of Mrs. Strombone. She's getting out of the hospital. Mom and I are going to spend the afternoon with her," I said. "Can't Eli go?"

"She has a piano competition."

"What about Stanley?"

"We're barely civil," she said. "And even if we were still together, he'd rather be run over by a car than sit in one with Gary." My friend looked like a squashed sunflower. She said, "I'm so alone, Dora."

"There are six and a half billion people on this planet," I said. "If anything, you're not alone enough."

She wasn't listening. She dropped her head in her hands and started blubbering in the hallway. Noel and Stanley happened by at that moment. Noel's incredible hazel eyes, the ones I'd taken long, leisurely swims in, locked with mine.

Noel took a step toward us. I'd willed him to, and he did. No matter what, Noel was a good, caring person who would always try to help his friends.

Too many of his friends were in need, though. Stanley, visibly rattled by the sight of Liza crying—he probably felt as helpless as she did—put his hand on Noel's shoulder and said what seemed to be "Leave it alone." Frowning, Noel broke eye contact with me and walked off with Stanley.

Twenty-two

"Can I get you something?" I asked. "Water? Aspirin? *Zoolander*? *Dodgeball*?"

Mrs. Strombone shook her head violently, which scared the crap out of me. Was she convulsing? In the throes of another attack? I backed away instinctively and called out, "Mom! Help!"

See, I hadn't completely lied to Liza. Mom had insisted that I sit with the patient for a spell. Mom must have been looking for a way out of the house. Dad was brooding in the office. Joya was locked in her room. It was tense. Bad enough to make Mrs. Strombone's dank apartment an attractive alternative.

Mom rushed into Mrs. Strombone's bedroom with a glass of water. She saw that the patient was agitated. "What did you do to her?" she asked.

"Nothing!"

Mom leaned over the bed and put her ear up close to Mrs. Strombone's mouth. The old woman croaked out the words "I . . . hate . . . Ben . . . Stiller."

Now I knew for sure she was senile. To Mom I said, "I offered to put on a DVD," and held up the choices I'd brought over from home.

"She's very cranky since the heart attack. Just sit with her, Dora," said Mom. "I'm trying to figure out some of her insurance paperwork and I need to concentrate."

"Why are you doing it?" I asked.

Mrs. Strombone closed her eyes and rolled onto her side.

Mom wagged her index finger to get me to join her in the kitchen. We took seats at the table. Forms and pink hospital receipts were piled high on it.

"I offered to do the paperwork," said Mom, "because no one else did."

"Where are her kids?" I knew Mrs. Strombone had three children. Their baby pictures were all over the place.

"Either dead, or 'dead to her,'" said Mom.

"Oh, yeah. I remember when her son died." Carl had been in a car accident around six years or seven years ago.

"Her daughter, Leslie, is a lesbian in Canada, and her living son, Carmine, married a black woman."

I said, "So Mrs. Strombone is a racist homophobe?"

"She's a product of her time and upbringing. She's also a lonely old woman and a good neighbor," said Mom. She sighed. "You must have realized by now that people are complicated. That one person can have both repellent and positive traits. Like a Nazi who rescues abandoned dogs."

"We exist on a shifting continuum," I said, nodding. "Pure evil on one side, pure good on the other. Most of us fall somewhere in the middle."

"I assume you're closer to pure good," said Mom.

"Of course," I assured her. "Maybe the heart attack sent Mrs. Strombone sliding toward pure evil?"

"Let this be a lesson to you, Dora. Intolerant people wind up alone and dying in a smelly room with no one to care for them."

"Except for the sucker who lives across the street," I said, smiling at Mom. She was an easy touch. No wonder she let Dad loan the leggy sitar poet all that money.

"A sucker and her sucker daughter," said Mom. "For the record, if you or Joya brings home a non-Jewish man—or woman—of any race or nationality, your father and I will be happy you've found someone to love."

I nodded. We were nearly the same height, and I probably weighed more than she did, but my mother was a much bigger woman than me.

"I don't want to die alone," I said. "I don't want to *be* alone."

"As long as I'm alive," said Mom, "you won't be."

A thump came from the bedroom. We both ran in to find that Mrs. Strombone had flung my DVDs across the room, cracking the boxes and scratching the discs.

Mom said, "The reviews are in."

★   ★   ★

"You look great," said Matt Greene. He was holding open the door to Stephanie's apartment with a sixty-watt smile.

This was a much better welcome than I'd received from Mrs. Strombone. Mom let me leave after an hour of sitting. The patient ignored me except for getting upset if I dared to open a book or flip through one of her ten-year-old copies of *Reader's Digest*. She wasn't happy unless I sat silently, staring straight ahead. Not at her. At the wall. The experience reminded me of her SAT prep class, and it was equally as educational. I almost fell asleep in the chair, sitting up, leaning to the side, jerking awake. A health care worker sent by her insurance company arrived. I was free to go.

I said to Matt, "You don't know how good it is to see a friendly face."

Matt helped me off with my hat and boots. My gloves, my scarf. He removed my parka. And then he unzipped my hoodie and started to unbutton my shirt. "Hey!" I said. "Not in the hallway."

"Then let's go in the back," he said, steering me down the long central corridor into the living room. "Mom and Liza won't be back for hours," he added, sitting me down on the couch.

We went at it with the making out. It felt good. But an element was missing. I didn't feel the same intensity as kissing in the empty planetarium theater. That had been out of this world. But now, with the bright daytime light, the lumpy couch, the lack of preliminary conversation, kissing felt too earthy. Too real and carnal. When Noel and I kissed, there was always an ethereal element, a magic glow.

Matt pulled me onto his lap and started to take off my shirt again. I watched his fingers at work. I was unafraid. But unmoved as well.

"I'm not afraid of sex," I announced, having the insight as I spoke the words. "I thought I was afraid of the physical part. Of wanting it too much or not wanting it at all. Of being bad at it. But now I don't feel afraid."

"Good to know," said Matt, pulling off his T-shirt.

"I've been avoiding the emotional risk," I said. "You present no risk. I don't love you. I have nothing to lose. Therefore, I have nothing to fear."

"So much the better," said Matt. "I don't love you either. But I do enjoy . . ."

"Spending time with me," I said.

"Exactly," he said, kissing between my bra cups.

"I'm wondering if emotionally risk-free sex has meaning, though," I said.

Matt sighed, frustrated. "We're going to have this conversation before anything happens, right?"

"Why do it if there's nothing between us?" I asked. "Except physical attraction."

"Except?" he asked. "Physical attraction is all that matters! It's a physical act, Dora."

"That's not what it felt like with Noel," I said. "Not that we did it. But it would have been . . . different."

"So go back to fucking Noel," he said, suddenly pissed

off. "Or not fucking Noel. Jesus, why did I bother with a seventeen-year-old?"

Matt pushed me off his lap and stood up. He yanked on his T-shirt and practically growled with annoyance, frustration, anger. For a hairy five seconds, I saw the potential danger of the situation. But Matt was trustworthy. At least, I was pretty sure he was.

I said, "The thing is, Matt, I don't want to die alone."

"Now you're afraid to die? You *were* afraid of sex, and now you're careening headlong to death. Let me concentrate on getting through the next five minutes," he snarled. "Then we can talk about everything that might potentially disturb you from this day forward, for the rest of your life."

"What happens in the next five minutes?" I asked.

"I calm down," he said.

Oh. Yes, well, the bulge in his jeans was a prominent distraction from our philosophical conversation. I suggested, "Perhaps you'd like to go masturbate in the bathroom?"

"Not funny, Dora."

"For the record, I had every intention of going through with it," I said. "But it just felt flat. I don't want my first time to be some meaningless, shallow act. Insert tab A into slot B. I guess I had to get close enough to doing it with you to figure that out."

"Sex should be meaningless!" he said. "Everything is meaningless! It's impossible to make a lasting, real impact on our species. Relationships, love, sex—none of it matters."

"So why do anything? Why go to college? Why make friends? Why have sex? Not that we are," I said.

"Because it feels good!" he blurted. He didn't say, "Duh!" but it was implied.

Matt was a reductive thinker. Relationships were spending time with someone. Sex was a way to feel good. His logic was simple and beautiful—and selfish and empty. He was older, but Matt Greene was not wiser.

I stood up. "Thanks, Matt. This has been really enlightening. I've got a lot to think about. The meaning of life. Or the meaninglessness of life. My head is way too full of ideas to have red-hot feel-good sex. So. Yeah. We're done."

"We're way past done, Dora," he corrected.

"I'm no longer your wedding date," I confirmed.

"We'll be on opposite sides of the room." He nodded.

Matt Greene, the same guy who sweetly pored over Joya's coloring books, was ejecting me from his life because I wouldn't put out. On the evil versus good continuum, at this moment in time, he was sliding fast toward asshole. He impatiently watched me re-zip my hoodie.

"Think you can move faster than evolution?" he asked.

Man, he was bitter. And a jerk of the highest order. I'd been blinded by his sun god brilliance. I should have known not to trust a guy who didn't ask first before he mauled me.

I had one boot on when the door burst open and Liza barreled into the apartment.

She saw Matt first, and screamed hysterically, "I jumped out of the car at a red light on 145th Street! I couldn't stand one more minute. They were telling me how great our life in Ossining is going to be. Matt, what am I going to do?"

Matt said, "Try growing up."

Here was a classic case of taking out one's hostilities on an innocent bystander. Matt was not only a nihilist; he was an asshole, too. Liza, as she was wont to do, dissolved into tears.

I went to her and put my arms around her. I said, "You're not alone, Liza. I'm here for you."

My blond pal lifted her head, focused swollen eyes at me, and said, "Dora? I thought you were at Mrs. Strombone's."

And that was the moment my gut clenched. I'd lied to her, and now she knew. I saw the realization process behind her eyes. She pushed my arms off and spun backward. "You promised you would stay away from Matt," she said.

"I will," I said. And this time I meant it.

To Matt she said, "I asked you to leave her alone."

He said, "I'm not accountable to you, Liza." Which was the college equivalent to saying, "You're not the boss of me."

Bastard! I hated Matt Greene with my bile ducts. I said, "We made a terrible mistake, Liza, but now we're BOTH going to concentrate on you."

"I don't want your attention! I don't want anything from you, or you, or Mom, or anyone!" she hurled at us. "Fuck you both, and fuck Brooklyn."

She tore into her room, rummaged and crashed around for a minute while I implored Matt to do something. She came out carrying a shoulder bag and left the apartment without saying another word.

"We have to go after her," I said to Matt.

"Right behind you," he said, flopping on the couch, turning on the TV.

I laced up in a flash, threw on my outer layers and tripped back into the Brooklyn winter. I ran down the street, around the block and all the way to the subway, into the Borough Hall station, up and down the platforms.

I couldn't find her. Liza was gone.

Twenty-three

"Where would she go?" asked Eli. After an hour's search mission around the neighborhood, I went straight to Eli's house. She was just back from her piano competition. (She won.)

"I'm calling Stanley," I said and did.

"Hey, Dora," he said.

"Have you seen Liza today?" I asked.

"Didn't she tell you? We broke up."

"Yes, I know that. But I thought she might come to you anyway."

He sighed. Stanley had friend fatigue. It was often tiring to be in Liza's support system. But, honestly, she had good reason to be upset this time. And Stanley wasn't the type of guy to shy away from a challenge. And Liza was a big one.

Stanley said, "Is she looking for me?"

He asked with both hope and fear. I was saved from answering his question when another call came in. I checked caller ID. Liza's home phone.

"Gotta go," I said to Stanley, clicking off and taking the new call.

To Eli I said, "It's Liza. She's home." Into my cell I said, "Hey!"

But it wasn't Liza's voice on the other end. Another hysterical, sniffling Greene female was on the line. "Dora, it's Stephanie Greene. Liza has disappeared. She jumped out of our car in Manhattan. I assumed she'd take the subway home. But she's not here."

"Did Matt say anything?" I asked.

"He's not here, either. I'm going out of my mind with worry! Is she with you?"

"No," I said. "I'm at Eli's. We're looking for her, too."

"You knew she was missing?" asked Stephanie, not too hysterical to put two and two together.

I swallowed hard and told Stephanie that I'd been with Matt, Liza found us together, freaked and ran off with a suitcase.

Stephanie listened quietly while I talked. When I finished, she asked coolly, "Where did she go?"

"I'm trying to find out."

"Call me when you do," she said and hung up.

I was now officially on the shit list of every member of the Greene family.

Eli, meanwhile, was shaking her head at me. She'd gotten the full story when I told Stephanie. "You just couldn't resist," she said. "What was it? His hair? The allure of the older man? That he was off-limits?"

"He made all the decisions," I said. "He took charge. I was just this stupid girl who went along, and I liked it. Until I really hated it."

"How could you have liked being treated like that for one split second?" asked Eli.

"Would it be idiotic to say I have no bloody idea?"

"Yes," said Eli.

"Stephanie Greene was on the phone with my mother for hours last night," I said to Eli at Chez Brownstone. "I heard Mom's end of it. Things like 'You were alone for a long time' and 'You are totally entitled to a little comfort and affection.' It was agony to listen to. I have no idea why I didn't lock myself in the bathroom." We were seated as far from anyone else as possible. We'd decided to keep Liza's disappearance to ourselves.

Eli said, "She called my mom, too."

"Mom told me Stephanie has filed a missing person's report with the police."

"Good," said Eli.

"I wonder why I'm not worried about her," I said. I had my suspicions about where Liza had run off to. I hadn't had a chance yet to confirm my theory, But I would, ASAP.

Eli said, "We know she's not going to walk through

Bed-Sty at three in the morning, waving a wad of cash. Liza was raised to be careful, just like we were. She's holed up somewhere safe, probably ordering room service right now."

"The ironic thing is, nothing happened with Matt! I was leaving. And *then* Liza catches us."

"But you lied to her," said Eli. "I'm not judging. Just telling it like it is."

Eric Brainard entered Chez Brownstone. He didn't see us in our secluded spot, and Eli didn't wave at him. He walked to the bulletin board on the wall by the food service area and hung up a poster.

I said, "What the hell?"

The words "Young Republicans Club" were written in huge red block letters, easily legible from any seat in the vast room. Eric made sure the poster was secure, and then he walked out of the cafeteria, staring straight ahead, with a faint smile on his lips. The second he was gone, a few kids threw farm-fresh cherry tomatoes at the poster. And bits of antibiotic free-range omelet. Someone hurled a slice of carrot cake, leaving a white-frosted smear.

"Play it again, Eli," I said, seated next to her on the piano bench in the music room. It was after three o'clock. We were alone.

" 'Romeo and Juliet'?" she asked, and started massaging the ivories. She went straight to the crescendo, the swelling, drippy notes of love.

"Did you see the Committee on Diversity poster? The one that went up next to Eric's?" I asked.

"And I quote," she recited, " 'Tolerance isn't just about race, religion and sexual orientation. It's about political preference, too. We have to respect the ideals of every student, regardless of his or her affiliation.' "

"You must have seen it when it first went up," I said. "It's illegible now. Totally splattered with organic produce."

"At Brownstone, you can be black, Asian, Latino, white, gay, transsexual, transvestite, Muslim, Catholic, Jewish. Anything goes," she said. "Except Republican."

I asked, "Where did I go wrong with Noel?"

"Liza is missing, and Eric Brainard has turned himself into the most hated kid in school. And you're thinking about old-news Noel."

"I'm glad Eric is spiraling downhill. Need I remind you, once upon a time, you hated him and his Asian fetish."

Eli played on. "I told him to go find himself a replacement. He can start at asiancutie.com."

So now they were over, too. Every newly happy couple had come undone in the span of one month. It was just February. The wedding was planned for Valentine's Day, less than two weeks away.

"Are you sad, happy, relieved, disappointed?" I asked Eli.

She said, "Yes."

The door opened. Jack Carp, come for his sheet music. He nodded at us.

I smiled at him brightly and nudged Eli in the ribs. She said, "Jack, did you know that Dora would love nothing more than to see us get back together?"

He dropped his black-leather-clad elbow on the piano and said, "Doesn't Dora have her own life to worry about?"

"Marry, she does," I said, standing up. "I'll leave you two to do whatever ex-boyfriend/girlfriends do when they find themselves suddenly available."

"Wait," said Eli, lifting her hands from the keys. "You asked me a question before."

Where I'd gone wrong with Noel. "What of it?" I said.

"I know how to figure it out."

"Tarot cards?"

"Ask Noel," said Eli as Jack took my place on the bench. Wordlessly, they launched into a duet.

I left them to their tune and plunged into freezing air. I ran home—only a few blocks—confirming the fact that I hated the cold even more than running.

I was two stoops away from my building when a hand grabbed my padded shoulder from behind. The Dropovs? No, the hand was bigger, stronger, male. My heart—already pounding from the jog home—nearly burst from my chest and out through the feathery confinement of my jacket. I might have had a heart attack. I might have pulled a Strombone.

I spun around, in self-defense mode, having learned to yell "No!" and jab an attacker in the eyeball—or the ball-ball—in seventh-grade health class. I would have done it, too, had he not squealed and doubled over to protect his jewels.

"Ben Teare?" I had nearly neutered Joya's boyfriend. "I could have killed you!"

"I doubt that, Dora," he said, recovering. "Look, I don't

have much time, and I've been waiting so long my nose is about to fall off. Just give this to Joya, okay?"

He forced a little box into my hand. A ring box. I started to open it, and he shrieked, "That's for her!"

"If you didn't want me to look, you should have wrapped it," I said, putting it in my pocket to examine later. "Consider it delivered."

"Thank you," he said.

"Why don't you just give it to her yourself?"

"You don't know?" he asked. I shook my head. "Our parents have forbidden us from seeing each other."

Joya's plunging grades would be enough for my parents to ground her. And Ben's priggish mom hadn't liked the libidinous direction of their relationship. They were being kept apart by family and denied their teenage love. Just like some fourteen-year-olds from Verona I happened to know about. Ben was asking me to be the go-between, to play the role of Nurse in real life.

I said, "You can still IM and text each other."

He said, "It's not the same."

I went into Joya's room, flinched at the mess. The piles of laundry, balled-up scraps of paper, books, magazines, pencils, pads, markers, a hundred Beanie Babies she refused to get rid of.

Joya was lying on her bed, reading her Spanish-language textbook. I tossed the ring box on her belly.

"From your secret admirer," I said.

"Matt Greene?" she asked. And then added, "No, Matt Greene is *your* secret love."

"Trust me, he's not." Anymore.

She opened the box. Inside, Ben had placed a green jawbreaker.

Instead of being happy or touched or however a fourteen-year-old should react at the sight of a large piece of candy, Joya started crying. She wasn't too upset to put the jawbreaker in her mouth and go to work on it, though.

I sat on the bed. God, I hated being cried to. "Joya, this is just a blip," I said. "You'll kick ass at school for two weeks, you'll get a few good grades and then Mom and Dad will loosen the chains."

"Two weeks!" she squealed.

"If you really loved him," I said, "you'd wait two years."

"You have no idea what you're talking about," she said. "You don't understand my pain."

"No one understands your pain," I said. "That's why it's yours."

"Mom and Dad are talking about testing, tutors. Templeton and Ratzenberger want me evaluated," said Joya. "They think I might have an 'attention issue.' I can see how this is going to play out, Dora. Shrinks. Pills. Hours in a locked room with a number two pencil."

"You don't have ADHD. You have a boyfriend," I said. Joya was terrified of standardized testing, had been since kindergarten. She'd been a slow reader. Resistant to math. Mom and Dad always said that if she could just keep up, she didn't need to worry. She was a "visual" thinker, not "verbal" or "mathematical."

The way I saw it, Joya had always been an oddball. "Quirky" was the commonly trotted-out euphemism to explain her failure to bond with other girls, her incessant, peculiar comic book drawings (I could see from the open sketch pad on her desk that she'd been working on "Mutant Babysitters IV"), the zombielike way she could zone out in front of the TV and not hear the phone ring or people calling her. It was weird. Maybe Joya did have a real problem. Worry for her hit me in the solar plexus.

I'd lasted one day as an island. That said a lot.

We sat quietly, the silence broken only by the *slurp-slurp* of Joya sucking the candy.

"So," I said, "Ben gives you a jawbreaker? Does that have any kind of sexual meaning?"

"Like what?" she asked, wide-eyed. "Ewww! You're disgusting." But she was grinning.

"I can't believe you didn't talk to me. About the grades," I said.

Joya switched cheeks and shrugged. "You would have called me stupid and lazy."

"Yeah, but I've been doing that for years," I said.

"I'm not pretending it doesn't bother me anymore," she declared.

"Okay, you're not stupid," I said. "But you are lazy."

"See? You don't want to help me. You just want to entertain yourself at my expense."

"Not true." It was true.

"Prove it," she challenged.

"How?"

"Say you're sorry," she insisted.

"You're sorry," I replied.

"Say 'I'm sorry.' "

I paused, picked up how serious she was. I said, "I am sorry, Joya."

She looked at me with her big brown wet eyes, like we'd just had a moment. I quickly stood up and walked to the doorway. "I'll deliver care packages to Ben if you want."

"Great!" said Joya, a smile spreading across her pixie face.

"Why don't you just give gifts to each other at school?" I asked, "logical" thinker that I was.

"Starting tomorrow, Mom is sitting in on my classes," she said. "It's beyond humiliating."

I'd heard tell of this cruel and unusual academic punishment. But never in my wildest nightmares did I think it could actually happen.

Mom at school. All day long. Shadowing her.

"It won't be bad," I said.

"It'll be worse," said Joya.

Twenty-four

That evening, I made an international phone call.

"Hello, is Liza there?" I asked.

"Who's this?" asked Ryan Greene, his voice crackling over the line from South Hampton, Bermuda.

"It's Dora Benet."

"Dora Benet! You sound grown-up! I haven't heard your voice in years," he said. "What's going on? How's Brooklyn?"

"Not to be rude, sir, but if you're up for small talk, that means you're not alarmed by the news that your daughter is missing, probably because you know where she is, perhaps sitting next to you, listening to your half of this conversation, waving her hands to signal that she doesn't want to talk to me. But she does, sir. So, if you please, put her on the phone."

"Hold on," he said.

Muffles. I was a cement mixer of emotion, churning with relief that I'd found her, awe that she'd traveled to another country, regret that my actions had sent her packing, and anger that she'd scared the shit out of us.

"Hello, Dora?" It was Ryan Greene again.

"Still here."

"Liza went to the club. She won't speak to you," he said. "But, believe me, I'll be speaking to her. She told me her mother sent her down here."

"And you believed her?" I asked, annoyed. "It's the middle of the school year."

"The way Liza explained it, Stephanie is so wrapped up in her wedding to this Gary Glitch character, she's neglecting Liza and wanted to get her out of the way."

"Stephanie would never neglect Liza," I said. "You know that!"

"Liza said she was under the influence of this Gary, who sounds like a Nazi. They want to force Liza to live in the suburbs? It's outrageous!"

I agreed on that point. But, jeez, if Ryan were a responsible parent, he would have called Stephanie as soon as Liza arrived. Then again, this was the man who chucked it all to move to an island.

I said, "Can I tell Stephanie that her daughter is safe?"

"I'll call her," he said.

"I don't like it," I said to Eli on the phone. I told her the Liza whereabouts story. A sense of foreboding roiled in my gut. Ryan telling Stephanie that he was harboring her fugitive daughter didn't have the makings of a happy catching-up conversation.

"Jack Carp and I are back together," said Eli.

"That was fast."

"I only did it to make you happy," she drawled.

"Does Eric Brainard know he's been replaced?"

"He'll have to wait for the press release."

"He might be moving on, too. If only in his delusional mind. Last week, I overheard a conversation between Matilda Rossi and Eric Brainard," I confessed.

"Overheard how?"

"I happened to be squeezed into a cranny behind the radiator in the teachers' lounge," I explained.

"Really," she said.

"Before school hours. Funny story, I dropped a quarter, and it rolled all the way up the stairs into the teachers' lounge, right into that tiny space, and I had to wedge myself in there to find it, and just then Ms. Rossi came in . . ."

"Stop," said Eli. "You were spying on Rossi because you hate her?"

"Sondra Fortune asked me to. She says Vin Transom broke up with her because he's hot for teacher."

"And she thought Rossi would go for that jockstrap? Sondra must be in love," ruminated Eli. "What did you overhear?"

"Eric going on and on about Rossi's gorgeosity. It was gross, Eli. And she asked him to do something. I don't know what. Double her column layout, I guess."

"Why didn't you tell me you were spying? Why didn't

you recruit me to help? You're keeping way too many secrets lately, Dora."

"Are you mad?" I asked.

"Not mad," she said. "Coldly plotting my revenge."

"On me?" I shuddered at the thought.

"Not you," she said. "On Ms. Matilda Rossi."

TO: Dora Benet
FR: Ms. Rossi
CC: Ms. Ratzenberger
Subject: Warning
Tuesday, February 7th, 2006, 7:30 A.M.
Ms. Benet:
    Please consider this an official warn-
ing. Your behavior in class is disruptive,
disrespectful and offensive. Your antics
detract from the learning experience for
the rest of your classmates. Also, your
homework and essay submissions have been
sub par. If your performance doesn't im-
prove drastically, I'm afraid I'll have to
send a formal letter to your parents and
put you on academic probation.
                        Regretfully,
                        M. Rossi

I read the e-mail during breakfast, only moments before Joya and I left for Brownstone—with our mommy. I hadn't walked to school with Mom since I was nine years old. Dad found my horror deeply amusing. He waved good-bye, still in his robe, chuckling madly, the best mood I'd seen him in since Patty O'Hearn, the metallurgist check bouncer, reappeared in his life. Maybe he was happy because he was getting time away from Mom. Couldn't say I blamed him.

We walked quickly in the cold, and I rushed ahead as we neared the building (no one saw me with her, whew). I didn't bother going to my locker. I marched straight up to Rossi's "office," still in my coat, to issue my formal objection to her formal warning. For once, there wasn't a line of boys waiting for an audience with her.

Hat-covered ear to the door, I heard voices inside. I knocked, but wasn't acknowledged. I reminded myself that her office, however Forbidden, was school property, paid for and maintained by my tuition fees.

I gripped the knob and pushed the door open. It creaked, predictably. But what I saw inside gave me the shock of my life (thus far).

Ms. Rossi was kneeling on the floor in front of her desk. Noel Kepner, my once and former Noel, was standing directly in front of her. From that angle, they were in a flagrantly inappropriate position. It appeared as if Ms. Rossi was going beyond her ordinary duties to the student body. Or, in this case, one student's body.

I definitely threw up in my mouth that time. I gagged and backpedaled, nearly fell down the stairs. I caught the banister at just the right moment, thank God, or Noel and Rossi *together* would have been my last sight on earth.

Noel caught me at the bottom of the steps. He got ahold of my parka and said, "Dora, wait!"

"Don't touch me!" I screamed.

"She dropped her pen on the floor and bent down to pick it up! You did not see anything, Dora."

I stumbled toward the girls' bathroom outside the cafeteria. "Don't tell me what I saw!" Granted, he was right. I hadn't actually *seen* anything. Just a split second. But a suggestive split second.

"What you saw was Ms. Rossi kneeling down to find her fucking pen!" he shouted, following me. Noel rarely raised his voice.

"Why were you there in the first place?" I asked. "Sucking up to the teacher? Or is it the other way around?"

He looked like I'd punched him in the kidney. "How could you think that of me?" he asked. "Do you know me at all?"

"I was going to apologize to you today," I said, leaning against the bathroom door. "I was going to beg you to give me another chance."

I escaped into the bathroom and then practically collapsed against the sinks.

A woman, just exiting one of the stalls, seemed startled to see me like that. She said, "Dora, my God, what's wrong?"

"Mom," I said, desperately happy to see her. She rushed over to me, kissed my forehead to check for fever. She put her hand on my cheek. Her care and concern pushed me over the edge. A curtain of tears poured out of my eyes and rolled down my face.

Mom seemed stricken. "Are you sick? Do you have chills?"

"I don't feel so good," I said, swooning.

"I'm taking you to the nurse's office right now."

The school nurse agreed: I was hot. I didn't remind anyone I'd been wearing my coat indoors for twenty minutes. I swore to Mom I'd be okay to walk the three blocks home on my own. I wasn't sick, really. But I was sickened. The sight of your sworn enemy's head orbiting your boyfriend's (ex's) crotch would do that to anyone.

I got to Garden Place, climbed up our stoop and reached into my bag for keys, which had gone missing. I put my bag on the snowy stoop and rummaged. I might have left the keys in another coat, or another bag. Since Mom and Dad were usually ALWAYS loitering inside, I never fretted about losing them. Dad was home. He'd let me in.

I buzzed. No response. Dad must have gone out. I tried calling home on my cell. No answer.

Standing there, shivering in the cold, I coughed. Great. I might be getting sick for real. What were my options? I couldn't go back to school. No way. Not ever. I didn't have enough cash for a movie. It would have to be Grind for coffee. I started down my stoop, glancing up and down Garden Place. My eyes landed on Mrs. Strombone's town house and I remembered: She and Mom had once exchanged keys for situations exactly like the one I was in now.

I walked across the street and buzzed at Mrs. Strombone's.

A pudgy middle-aged black woman let me in—Ms. Fitzsimmons, the health care worker I'd met the other day. I reintroduced myself and explained my situation.

She said, "You can wait here if you want."

"The thing is, Mrs. Strombone has a spare set of keys for my apartment," I said.

"Any idea where she keeps them?"

"No."

"Good luck finding them," she said, letting me inside. "She won't tell you where they are. She hasn't said a single word to me in a week."

"I'm sure she appreciates your being here," I said.

Ms. Fitzsimmons smiled knowingly and said, "Right."

The patient was awake in her stuffy bedroom. I tiptoed to the side of the bed and said, "Hello, Mrs. Strombone. It's Dora Benet, from across the street."

"The Hebe?"

From the room's threshold, Ms. Fitzsimmons guffawed.

"The Hebe's daughter, actually," I said. "But, yeah, also Hebe."

"My address book," said the crone. "On my night table. Get it!"

I jumped to comply. Finding the tattered leather address book, I said, "Do you happen to remember where you might have put a spare set of keys to my house?"

"Call Leslie."

"Leslie?"

"The lesbian. In Canada."

I opened the book and found the L's. Sure enough, there

were a few numbers for "Leslie," including one that went with an address in Montreal.

I said, "Your estranged daughter?"

"Call her!" insisted Mrs. Strombone with surprising force. "Do it now. Before you kill me."

Not seeing a phone by the bed, I used my cell and dialed the number. It rang a few times, and then a soft female voice answered, "Fuse Box."

Fuse Box? I said, "Hello. Is this Lesbian? *Leslie!* Is this Leslie Strombone?"

Ms. Fitzsimmons said, "Smooth."

Warily, the woman on the phone asked, "Who is this?"

"My name is Adora Benet. I live on Garden Place in Brooklyn. Across the street from your mother. She asked me to call you."

The patient whispered. "Tell her I'm near death."

I said into the phone, "Is this Leslie?"

"Yes," she answered.

"Your mother is near death."

Leslie asked, "How near?"

Mrs. Strombone asked, "What'd she say?"

The old woman clearly hoped her daughter was upset. She wanted to spread her misery all the way to Montreal.

"She's one foot in," I reported into the phone. "And that's why your mom wants to make amends. She's sorry for being such a small-minded, nasty bigot her whole life. She accepts you and loves you for who you are, and she wants to see you again before she kicks."

Mrs. Strombone's eyes bulged. She clutched her heart, and Mrs. Fitzsimmons stepped forward to take her pulse.

Leslie, meanwhile, asked, "Did she really say that, or are you putting words in her mouth?"

I said, "Here she is," and handed the phone to Mrs. Strombone, who grabbed it with the hand not holding her chest.

She warbled, "Leslie?"

Hearing the sound of her daughter's voice took twenty years off the old woman's face. She said, "Yes" once and then handed the phone back to me. I pressed it to my ear. Leslie had hung up.

I asked, "Is she coming?"

Mrs. Strombone nodded.

"You're welcome," I said. "Now, about those keys."

Triumphant, I crossed the street, spinning the keys in my fingers. A tall, slim woman was walking down my side of the block, seemingly right for me. We got to my stoop at the same time. We took the steps in tandem. I waited for her to push a buzzer, see which apartment she was looking for.

She pressed the button for the upper duplex. My place. I smiled at her, and she returned it. No answer on the intercom.

I said, "May I help you?"

She gave me her full attention. Up close, I could see she was about my parents' age. In her day, she must have been quite a dish, with razor-sharp cheekbones, auburn hair and lush lips. She looked like the model Christy Turlington, but worn out, like she'd seen many more late nights than early mornings.

"You must be Adora," she said in a scratchy smoker's growl.

"And you are Patty," I said, "coming to see my father when my mother is out."

She smiled gamely. "You look just like your dad," she said. "But you take after your mom."

And what was that supposed to mean? I smiled back, going for sinister. "Dad isn't home. But I'd be happy to give him a message."

Patty reached into her cheap knit tote and removed a manila envelope. "For the record," she said, "he invited me."

She walked down the steps, up the street and out of sight without looking back once.

I opened the envelope. It was stuffed with cash. A thick stack of hundred-dollar bills.

I'd always had a fantasy of someone coming up to me on the street and inexplicably handing me an envelope full of cash. I could now cross that off my list.

Using my key, I went inside, where I could examine the stack up close, fan it, shuffle it, flip it in my ear. I took the building's steps two at a time and burst into the empty apartment.

Except it wasn't empty. Sitting at the dining room table, Dad was dressed in his stay-at-home writer outfit of Levi's and a flannel shirt, white T, bare feet. He seemed stunned by my entrance. On the table in front of him: a pot of fresh-brewed coffee and two mugs.

"Expecting someone?" I asked. Then I remembered: The intercom was broken. He hadn't heard me or Patty buzz.

"Dora!" he blurted. "What are you doing home?"

"You invited Patty O'Hearn over here behind Mom's back," I said accusingly.

He blinked at me. "Careful, Dora."

"Did Mom know about your *date*?" I asked.

Dad stood up so abruptly that his chair fell over with a resounding thud. His face turned red as a beet. His mouth twitched with fury. "No parties, no dates, no allowance, no nothing, until further notice," he raved.

Ed Benet, by the way, was Mr. Even Keel. A mellow dude. His head was so level, you could rest a Diet Coke on it. I hadn't expected him to get this angry. So I'd accused him of deceiving Mom. Well, I guess that was pretty bad.

But I was just as angry. At him, Noel, Matt, Rossi, everyone and everything.

I'd had it. Oh, I could pretend to absorb the blows. But try as I might, I was not made of sponge.

I ran up to my room, grabbed the one thing I needed from my desk drawer, slammed back downstairs and out the apartment door. Dad yelled after me, stomped down the steps behind me, even chased me out onto the street. But I was faster than him. Way faster and lighter.

The cash-stuffed manila envelope hadn't weighed me down a bit.

Twenty-five

"Welcome to Bermuda National Airport," said the flight attendant into the airplane PA system.

Since the evening flight was nearly empty, I whiled away the two hours counting my cash.

After I'd paid for the taxi to LaGuardia airport, the magazines and dinner I bought there, the American Airlines ticket, and a mini shopping spree of bathing suits and sunglasses, I had $4,689.54 left. I kept the receipts in the envelope with the cash. By now, Mom knew I'd run away. If she searched my desk, she'd see that my passport was missing. Dad might have figured out that I ran into Patty O'Hearn on the street. That she'd given the envelope to me.

I'd wait until tomorrow to call. They'd be so glad I wasn't

dead in a gutter or a ditch, they'd forgive me for stealing the money and running away to paradise.

American money, I soon learned, was universally accepted in Bermuda. I got in a taxi at the airport and asked to be taken to the Fairmont Southhampton Princess in South Hampton.

Liza had described the golf and beach club where her dad worked so many times, it was almost familiar when we pulled up the steep driveway to the main hotel building. The hotel reminded me of Southern Civil War–era plantation mansions (think Tara in *Gone with the Wind*) except it was painted pink with creamy trim. Hibiscus trees with bright orange and red flowers were planted around the building, along with giant impatiens and other enormous plants I didn't know the names of. Everything, from the trees to the grass, was lush, overgrown, green, exuding oxygen, making my skin tingle. The night was clear, the moon high, stars bright. The evening air was cool. Not nearly as hot as I'd expected. But warm enough that I had to carry my parka, hat, gloves and scarf.

A porter came out of the hotel to greet me. I let him guide me inside to the lobby. The space was open-air and breezy, with tropical flower arrangements—lilies and birds of paradise—everywhere I looked. Potted palm trees grew in gold planters. The stucco walls, seashell pink, matched the abundant drapery and throw rugs. The lounge furniture had that island flair, lots of lacquered wicker and bamboo themes, with pink and orange cushions.

For all the vivid colors and tropical bombardment, the lobby seemed sparse. I wasn't sure why, exactly, until I walked straight up to the concierge desk and four hotel employees rushed to help me.

The place was practically empty. Only a few guests seemed to be milling about, all of them gray-haired couples in their seventies.

I smiled at the meticulously neat black woman at the concierge desk. "Do you have any rooms?"

"Sure do," she said. "This is our off-season."

I didn't get it. "But it's Bermuda."

"In February," she said. "Too cold to swim or snorkel. Too windy for tennis and golf."

Yikes. No snorkeling? Did that mean no Ryan Greene? Maybe he went to another club during the off-season.

Besides that, I'd paid a hundred dollars for a new bikini at the airport.

I asked, "Do you know a snorkel boat guide named Ryan Greene?"

She smiled, her teeth blindingly white, and said, "Of course!"

"Is he around?"

"He lives in a house on the beach, by the dunes."

She gave me detailed directions (which involved a shuttle bus ride to the beach club, which was closed, and a mile walk on the sand).

I decided I'd go tomorrow. For now, I checked into the hotel. I got myself a luxury room, with a minibar and a Jacuzzi, for the off-season discount price of two hundred a night. I wasn't sure if that was a bargain or not. I ordered room service for dinner: crab cakes and a green salad, a liter of Diet Coke and a slice of coconut cake. The bill was eighty-five dollars.

I decided not to call my parents tomorrow, either. At these prices, they'd need to be really, really worried before I got in touch.

Elbow Beach, where, ironically, my parents spent their honeymoon all those years ago, had pink sand, soft and fluffy as baby powder. I took off my clogs to walk barefoot (otherwise, I was wearing my jeans and sweater from yesterday). I put a toe in the waves as they washed up on the beach. Freeeezing. But the blue-green color, at once bright and dark, and the smell of salt and sea mitigated the sting of cold. The air temperature was like New York in May. Steaming, glorious sunshine warmed my face and feet. My hair whipped around in the breeze—which was both romantic and tragic. If I were to live here, I'd have to shave my head like a lamb, or suffer chronic, uncontrollable frizz. No amount of gel could contain the maximizing puff of tropical humidity, even during the off-season. I cared only theoretically.

I walked for half an hour, a mile of primo beach, and didn't see another soul. It was just me and sand. Me and sun. Me and the sea. I thought fleetingly of Noel, of walking with him through all this natural beauty. And then I remembered the last time I'd seen Noel, and the sunshine feeling whipped away on the wind.

The concierge gave good directions. I found Ryan Greene's beach house. I'd have called it a "beach hut" or "beach hovel."

On a bad day, one might go as far as "beach shanty." I couldn't imagine Liza spending a night there. One big gust of wind, and the shaky shelter would topple. The roof had a few loose tiles. The lime green door was splintered. A pink and blue ferryboat was tethered to the mooring. Leaning upright against the house was a gray rubber dinghy. On the house's rickety porch, there was a rubber garbage can full of flippers, masks and snorkels soaking in seawater.

I knocked on the door.

Someone shouted, "Be right there!"

A man's voice. And then there he was. Ryan Greene. Or, a man who closely resembled the Ryan Greene I'd known, the clean-shaven, slightly plump, prison-pallor, buttoned-up Wall Streeter who'd driven away from Hicks Street three years ago in a rented U-Haul. The slim guy in the doorway had scruffy sun-bleached blond hair, a desert-island blond beard, skin tanned as a strap of leather. He wore torn jeans, a faded yellow sweatshirt and no shoes. His feet were as tan as his face.

"It can't be," he said, grinning, glass blue eyes (a match for Liza's) sparkling like the sun on the ocean.

"I'm afraid it is," I said.

"Dora! Come on in!" he said, drawing me into the pile of sticks he called home.

Inside, the place looked more hospitable. I wasn't familiar with beach house terminology, but if I were to advertise the place as a listing in the Sunday *Times*, I'd describe it as a four-hundred-square-foot studio with galley kitchen, original beams, ocean views. Ryan's bed was covered with a tangerine fleece blanket and five big, cushy pillows. His couch was coral pink and draped with a baby blue blanket. There was electricity. Chinese lanterns hung from the rafters on the ceiling. His desk had a phone and an Apple iBook (circa 2003). The kitchen was little more than a four-burner stove, oven, microwave, sink and minifridge. A small table had four chairs around it. In one of those chairs sat Liza, glaring at me.

She said, "I'm not going home."

I sank onto the couch. "Neither am I."

Ryan said, "The more the merrier."

Turning to him, I said, "You went Jimmy Buffett."

Liza said, "Who?"

"We'll find some room for you, Dora. But I need to ask," he said, "do your parents know you're here?"

"Of course they do! And you won't have to squeeze me in. I'm staying at the hotel."

Liza continued to glare at me. She wasn't done being mad yet. I decided to let her process my arrival before trying to apologize. I said, "Sorry to interrupt you. I can see you're busy."

They appeared to be doing absolutely nothing.

"Why don't you come to the hotel later?" I asked. "For dinner. The Coral Reefer? At five?"

Ryan whistled through his teeth. "Pricey," he said.

"On me," I said.

Liza sniffed, "We have previous plans."

Ryan looked at her beseechingly. I could tell he was feeling the strain of Liza in her dark mood.

"I'll be there anyway," I said, and left the bungalow, shack, hut, whatever.

I counted to ten and looked back. No Liza running down the beach to beg me to come back. I hadn't really expected her to. She wasn't much of an athletic person. That said, all this outdoor splendor had been good for her. She'd definitely lost a pound or two since she left Brooklyn.

The sun rose. By noon, it was high and hot. I stopped trekking near the hotel's beach club. I sat on the sand, looked out at the horizon and let my mind go blotto in the movement of waves.

I fell asleep for a few minutes and woke up with sand in my mouth. Upon returning to the hotel, I took a hot bubbling Jacuzzi bath. I noshed out of the minibar. I did a lap with the TV remote control. Paradise—who knew?—was actually kind of boring and lonely.

I resisted the temptation for as long as I could stand it— about ten minutes. Then I dialed my cell.

"Hello?"

"Joya," I said, "it's me."

I'd called her cell, assuming that my parents were monitoring the landline closely.

"Hello," she said, clipped and terse.

"I'm in Bermuda," I said.

"I'm sorry, you have the wrong number," she said.

"Tell Mom and Dad I called, but that I refused to pinpoint my exact location. I'm fine, with friends, and I'll come home when I'm good and ready."

"No, this is not Larry's Rent-a-Wreck," she added.

The phone muffled. "Dora?" screamed my mom. "Where the hell are you? Your father is sorry! Do you hear me? He's sorry!"

Mom must have snatched Joya's phone out of her hand. I pictured them sitting on the couch in the living room, their three cells and the landline on the table, waiting for one to ring.

"I'm sorry, too," I said. "Tell him."

"Wait!" she shouted. "Wait! Do you still have chills? Drink a lot of flui—"

I hung up.

I was sorry. Sorry I'd kissed Matt, betrayed Liza, accused Dad, scared Mom, hectored Joya. The only thing I wasn't sorry about was walking in on Noel and Rossi. Those two could have their March/May affair, their illegal-in-twenty-states romance.

I simmered in my own jealous juices until five. Dinner couldn't have come soon enough. I zipped down the elevator to the lobby restaurant, the Coral Reefer, and got a window table in the nearly empty space. Liza and Ryan hadn't shown up. I waited a few minutes and then ordered a cocktail: shrimp. Extra Tabasco in the sauce. No matter how depressed and lonely, I could always eat.

"Is this seat taken?"

Liza vaporized like a cloud in a peasant skirt and a pink polo shirt.

"I thought I'd have to drown my sorrows in shrimp by myself," I said. She slid into the chair next to mine. "No Ryan?"

"He had things to do. Snorkels to clean, sand to sweep."

I nodded. She nodded back. The waiter broke the silence by noisily serving my appetizer on a silver plate.

"Nice place," I said. "Your dad's shack. *Home!* His lovely home."

"I'm waiting," she said, sampling my eighteen-dollar dish.

I said, "I'm sorry! How many days, how many ways, can I say the same fucking thing? I stole five thousand dollars from my parents and flew all the way down here to apologize. So accept it, or you can buy your own dinner."

"Okay," she said, moving the plate in front of her. "I accept your apology. But you're crazy if you think three little shrimp qualifies as dinner."

I signaled the hovering waiter and ordered lobster bisque, conch fritters, crab cakes, scallops in bacon and clams casino. We slurped shellfish until we were stuffed. While we ate, I filled her in on the events leading up to my impromptu vacation. Telling her, in the joyful frenzy of our feast, made it all sound silly, comic, ridiculous. We were howling by the time I got to my description of Dad chasing me down Garden Place in his bare feet. "How'd he get back inside?" she asked. "If he left the apartment without his keys."

I hadn't thought of that. "He might have been stranded outside, in bare feet."

We looked at each other and snort-laughed until dizzy.

I signed the bill to my room (I almost didn't dare look: $187!). Holding hands, we lumbered out of the hotel, down the long, winding stairway cut into a cliff and wound up on the fluffy pink beach.

We walked in silence for a few minutes until we came to a stop, right by my napping spot. We flopped on the sand. The sun was setting, but still bright, over the horizon.

Liza said, "I've spent the last three days sitting here, staring at the ocean." The waves were hypnotic. "I know you've been listening to Matt lately. The vast universe and meaninglessness of our existence. He talks about our insignificance to make himself sound important. It's his way of impressing girls. And you fell for it."

I said, "He's gorgeous, too."

"He highlights his hair," she said. "He self-tans."

"I suspected that," I said. "Streaks on his stomach."

Liza grimaced. "Don't tell me that!"

"So you were trying to keep me away from Matt to protect me?"

"And hog you for myself," she said. "And I was sad about Noel."

That comment gave me a pang. He'd asked, "Do you know me at all?" I did, once. I really did.

Liza threw a shell at the waves. "Matt says when you look at the stars you seem small," she said. "Dad thinks when you look at the ocean, your *problems* seem small. That's why I came down here."

"Except your problems aren't small," I said.

"My dad hasn't been on a date since he moved," said Liza. "That's three dateless years. With tourists parading in front of him like a beauty pageant, looking for a vacation fling with a local. And you've got to admit he has a certain island charm.

Dozens of women must have hit on him. And he never took the opportunities. Doesn't that tell you something?"

I smiled. "This conversation isn't about you, you, you, is it?"

"No, no, no," she said.

"You knew if you ran away to Bermuda, your dad would have to bring you back to Brooklyn. And then he'd see your mom again."

Liza smiled wickedly, the setting sun shimmering across her newly bronzed skin. I was awed by her beauty. Liza was radiantly in her element.

"Finding you and Matt together pushed me to do it, to run away," she said. "I was upset that you lied. But I was glad for the excuse."

"So you were pretending to be mad at me this morning," I said.

"I had to put on the show," she said. "Refuse to go home, so Dad would have to drag me back himself. He hasn't even brought up taking me home, though. But now you're here— and I'm so glad you are. We can do stupid island things like steal beers from the club bar and flirt with beach bums. Or go swimming naked."

"Let's do it!" I said, standing up, pulling off my top (which, after a couple of days, was starting to stink).

"I meant in the pool!" she said. "The ocean is too cold."

"Wimp," I said, peeling down my jeans. "Come on! The beach is deserted."

"Dora," she said, her blue eyes wide at me in my underwear, "you look good. I think your boobs are bigger."

"Here goes everything," I said, thumbs in my panties.

Liza shrieked when I pulled them down. I threw my bra at her, and ran bare-assed into the ocean.

Early reports were correct: The water was freezing. Nonetheless, I waded in, up to my hips. Legs numb, I dove into the waves. When I surfaced—every inch of my skin tingling from salt and cold—I saw Liza's lush nakedness charging toward the water.

She dove in, surfaced, sputtering, screaming.

I said, "I feel reborn! Like I've returned to the primordial ooze from whence I came!"

Liza splashed me and proclaimed, "A baptismal cleansing of the soul!"

"A Druid ritual of purification!"

Liza said, "I always knew you were Druish."

We frolicked like drunken dolphins until our lips turned blue. Teeth chattering, cupping our tits, we trudged out of the ocean into air that seemed colder than the water.

We grabbed our clothes and ran the quarter mile to Ryan's shack. We liberated some towels from the clothesline and went inside, laughing hysterically.

Ryan was at his desk. He heard us come in and looked up with a confused smile. When he realized we were naked under the towels, the man who'd bathed us as toddlers and changed our shitty diapers turned bright red under the tan.

Liza said, "We just had the best time! We went skinny-dipping, and some local guys guarded our clothes for us. Wasn't that nice of them? And then they gave us beer and offered us pot and coke, since they had so much for themselves."

"We refused," I said. "But they were so cool, we agreed to meet them for dinner tomorrow night at their house." To Liza, I said, "How old do you think they were?"

She pursed her lips and said, "Not too old. Around thirty?"

Ryan stared in shock, apparently on the verge of a massive Strombone. He choked and then stumbled out of the house, knocking over the garbage can of snorkels, getting soaked in seawater. He yelled at us to lock the door, stay inside and that he'd be right back, no doubt off to pummel the first beach-comber he found.

While we dressed in some ratty T-shirts and surf shorts, Liza said, "Twenty bucks says we're on a plane by noon tomorrow."

She got that wrong.

We were in the air by seven a.m. Ryan cleaned up nice for the trip back to New York. He'd shaved, which left a funny tan line on his cheeks, and trimmed his own hair (nicely). He wore clean trousers, a white shirt, charcoal wool coat—and sneakers. He sat between us on the plane and fidgeted with his earphones the entire trip.

Liza, on the aisle, asked, "Is Mom meeting us at the airport?"

Ryan croaked, "Yes."

From the window seat, I asked, "Are you nervous to see Stephanie?"

Ryan ignored the question and said, "Your parents will be at the airport, too."

"I was afraid of that," I said.

Twenty-six

A Brooklyn Winter's Tale
Week V, Scene I
Mom and Dad's home office, Wednesday late afternoon

"Count it," said Mom. She was next to Dad in their his-and-her chairs. Behind her, the iMac screen glowed, casting its blue light onto her hardened face.

I counted out hundred-dollar bills into her open palm. "Thirty-eight, thirty-nine, forty. Okay, that's four thousand. Plus one, two twenties, four dimes and three pennies."

Mom folded the $4,040 in half and slipped the bills into her pocket. She said, "I'll give you the change. You owe me nine hundred and sixty bucks."

I could tell she meant it. I gulped. "Where am I going to get that kind of money?"

"A job," she stated like she had it all figured out.

"What about my homework?" I whined. "My SAT prep?"

"Your mother and I have discussed it," said Dad, who hadn't looked me in the eye once, not at the airport, on the tense cab ride home or at the midday meal. "You're going to work for us."

"What do I have to do?" I asked, daunted.

Mom said, "You're going to handle our overflow reader e-mail." I assumed she was talking about the letters that were sent to their *New York Moon* column mailbox. Of the hundreds of e-mailed Q's they received each week, they supplied A's for only a few. The rest, well, I'd never thought about what happened to them.

"Read each e-mail. Search our archives for previously published answers that might apply and send one to the reader. If you can't find something from our archives, send the 'thanks for your interest, we can't answer all e-mails personally' response."

"That'll take hours!" I bellowed.

Many of their readers asked questions about sex. The last thing I wanted to do was crawl though my parents' archives about their erotic tips and tricks.

Mom said, "Tough. We'll pay you a hundred fifty dollars for a week."

"Six weeks!" I groaned.

"And two days," calculated Dad. "Starting today."

They nodded at each other. On cue, they both stood up. Mom fiddled with the mouse and clicked her way to their column e-mail queue. She showed me the archives search command.

I asked, "Am I forgiven?"

Dad said, "Ask again in six weeks and two days."

Week V, Scene II
Grind, early Thursday morning

"Pass the Splenda," said Liza. "This needs to be sweeter."

I gagged. She was drinking a caramel mochaccino, which was already as sugar rich as a Reese Witherspoon movie marathon.

"Tell me about the Ryan/Stephanie reunion," said Eli, adding a heaping spoonful of raw sugar to her coffee.

Liza said, "Awkward. Mom was waiting at the airport. After she hugged me, she thanked Dad for bringing me home. They didn't fall into each other's arms and declare the renewal of their love, as I'd hoped. But I sensed something went on between them."

"Definitely," I agreed. "My parents commented on it in the taxi home."

"What'd they say?" asked Liza, rapt. She'd always lapped up my parents' advice pudding.

"When Ryan and Stephanie greeted each other, they didn't touch," I said. "No polite cheek kiss, no friendly handshake. No sock on the arm like old chums. They kept their hands and lips to themselves. If they felt nothing for each other, they'd have touched palms. Dad said that touching palms is the universal, cross-cultural, aeons-old, instinctual friendly greeting of choice in primates. No palm touch can mean only one thing."

"That Stephanie and Ryan are not primates?" asked Eli snidely.

"They're not friends," I corrected.

Liza clapped her palms together in glee. "All according to my master plan!" she sang. Eli and I nodded politely, as if Liza had the ability to plan life beyond where to have lunch.

Eli asked, "Did Stephanie cry when she saw you?"

"Do fish swim?" I said.

"Did Liza cry when she saw Stephanie?" asked Eli.

"Do birds fly?"

"I can't help it!" pleaded Liza, laughing, in her best mood since October. "So, Eli," she said, "what'd I miss?"

"Eric and I broke up," Eli announced with the passion of a wet mop.

"Are you okay?" asked Liza, damp in the eye. "You were in love with him at one point."

Eli shrugged. "That was before I found out he was in the Bush League."

"The what?" asked Liza.

We explained the developments of the last two days. I said, "Weird how Asian fetishist Eric is attracted to Matilda Rossi."

"When he did that first cover story about her, I said something like, 'At least she's not your type.' And Eric said, 'She's every guy's type.' Anyway, I've decided to swear off boys for the next few months."

"What about Jack Carp?" I asked.

"We tried for a day, but then decided not to move backward in time," said Eli.

Liza said, "You can't turn your heart on and off like that!"

"*You* can't," said Eli. "I can."

She could. Eli had superhuman emotion control. Managing matters of the heart was her special skill. I'd long suspected that, one day, Eli would meet a man who would blow her away, wrench her out of control. That man would be the great love of her life. Which isn't to say he'd be the man she married. Eli might like getting swept away by a man for a short while. But no way would she be able to live with it.

I said, "Five weeks ago, we sat at this table, congratulating ourselves for being in three solid relationships. And now look at us."

Liza said, "The two of you look pretty good to me."

"And you," I said, catching the wave of her sunshine. "You are beautiful."

"We've each lost about one hundred and fifty unwanted pounds," said Eli, who glanced at the door. "Don't look. Three hundred of those lost pounds have just walked into Grind."

I held up my spoon and saw the upside-down fun house reflection of Noel and Stanley. They were walking toward our table. I kept my eyes front, on Eli. She watched the boys' progress through the café, her black eyes locked on them coldly.

Thank God Eli was my friend. Otherwise, she'd scare me shitless.

"Hello, Dora," said the familiar voice, right behind me.

I drew a deep breath and turned around. Noel smiled hesitantly. I said, "Hey."

"Walk with me to school?" he asked.

Eli and Liza's eyebrows went up, as if pulled by strings. Wordlessly, I stood, put on my coat and flung my bag over my shoulder. To my friends I said, "Expect my full report via e-mail."

Stanley took my place at the table, which made Eli groan and Liza squirm.

I rushed outside. Noel scrambled after me. Double-timing at my side, he said, "I heard you and Liza ran away to Bermuda. I feel responsible."

"That had nothing to do with you," I lied.

"What you saw in the teachers' lounge—"

I held up my glove to stop him. "Has been surgically removed from my memory. An experimental procedure. Performed only in Bermuda."

He smiled. "So you did leave because of me."

I groaned. "I haven't told a soul about it, if that's what you want to know. Except for Liza and Eli. But that was therapeutic."

Noel looked nervous. Splotches colored his cheeks, contrasting with his fair skin and gray-today eyes. He wasn't wearing a hat, and the tops of his ears were dark pink under the mink brown hair I once loved to play with, twisting it around my finger, fastening it in tiny ponytails.

"It's my fault," he said. "What happened to us. I started the breakup ball rolling, and then it just picked up speed. Straight downhill."

I said, "You expect me to disagree?"

"We never really talked about it," he said.

"I know how that must kill you," I said.

We'd arrived at Brownstone and loitered outside. We were both waiting for some kind of declaration or apology from the other. I flashed back to the scene at the airport. Stephanie and Ryan, not touching, not looking at each other. I stole a peek at Noel, at the face I'd kissed every quarter inch of, the eyes that had been a tranquil ocean to me.

He said, "I wish I could stop feeling bad. It's like a hole in my gut that won't go away."

"You have guilt," I said. "There is one thing you could do to make it up to me."

"What?" he asked limply.

"Give me nine hundred and sixty dollars," I said.

Week V, Scene III
Chez Brownstone, Thursday afternoon

"Yes, Mother," I grunted.

"You don't have to grunt," said Mom, who, as part of my punishment for running away from home on a school night, commanded me to have lunch with her at Chez Brownstone while Joya was in gym class. She was now demanding to know if the lasagna on the menu was made on the premises.

"And don't call me 'Mother,' " she added. "It makes me sound old."

"You are old," I said. "As in, 'too old for this *beep*.' "

I glanced at the stairs to the teachers' lounge, which were, as usual at this hour, crowded with pubescent devotees of Matilda Rossi. I'd thought Ms. Ratzenberger was going to put a stop to her fan club activity. I made a mental note to send an anonymous e-mail to the upper school director later today, complaining about the fire hazard (although I'd like to see that stairway burn).

Mom and I both got the lasagna. She carried her tray to a table in the middle of the room, where Kim Daniels and other members of the Teeming Masses were eating and gossiping about the Ruling Class girls who hated them.

Kim saw me and Mom, and waved us over. "HELLO, Dora. HELLO, Mrs. Benet. It's so GREAT to see you."

"Hello, dear," said Mom, who was struggling to remember who this girl was. Everyone knew my parents, of course. Their picture was in the *Moon* every Monday.

Kim said, "So, what BRINGS you to Chez BROWN-STONE today, Mrs. Benet?"

I kicked Mom under the table. Anything that was said to Kim Daniels was telegraphed round the school within an hour. Mom opened her mouth to reply, but she didn't get a chance to say a single word.

The door to the teachers' lounge suddenly burst open, smashing a few ninth-grade boys at the landing. Two whirling figures tumbled out of the lounge, hitting, yanking at each other, shoving. Two boys.

Kim Daniels bellowed, "FIGHT!!"

The two boys rolled down the stairs, taking a few of the other Rossi acolytes with them. The fighters crashed at the bottom and continued to pummel each other. Students had leapt up on benches to see the fight. There was cheering, some clapping.

It turned out that Mom had picked an excellent table. We had front-row seats for the action.

Despite our prime viewing spot, Mom screamed, "What's going on?"

Vin Transom and Eric Brainard were beating the crap out of each other. That was plain. I yelled back, "Move the tray!"

No sooner had the words exited my mouth than Vin threw Eric on top of my tray, smushing the back of his head into my plate of lasagna. Then Vin grabbed my Snapple and emptied it on Eric's face.

Mom leapt back, away from the table, her hands on either cheek in shock. She yelled, "Vin Transom! Stop that this instant!"

He glanced up at her and snarled (!). The two-second distraction was enough for Eric to squirm free, reach over his head to grab the square of lasagna from Mom's tray and fling it with excellent aim at Vin Transom's pie hole.

Mom screamed, "Eric Brainard! You're going to pay for that!"

Mr. Contralto appeared suddenly. He grabbed the boys by the backs of their neck and lifted them off the ground.

The boys jerking in his grip, he turned to Mom and asked, "Pardon me, ma'am. Who started it?"

Mom, flustered, said, "I'm not sure."

Mr. Contralto frowned. He was only too eager to mete out punishment to the guilty.

Mom threw in, "But they both showed complete disregard to other people's property."

"I'm taking them to Ms. Ratzenberger's office."

"I'm coming with you," said Mom, calming down and shifting into helper mode. "If we sit down and discuss our problems like adults, I'm sure we can settle this without violence."

Neither boy had yet to say a word. Mr. Contralto lowered them and shoved them toward the exit. "Move," he barked.

Vin and Eric moved. Mr. Contralto and Mom followed.

Everyone in the cafeteria watched them walk out, lasagna meat and sauce dripping off the back of Eric Brainard's head like brains and blood.

I was, perhaps, the only person in the room not staring after them. I was looking up, to the top of the Stairway to Hell. Matilda Rossi stood on the landing, motionless, expressionless, except for a small, sly smile on her lips.

Week V, Scene IV
English lit classroom, Friday morning

" 'I saw the wound, I saw it with mine eyes, here on his manly breast,' " I read, from my Oscar-worthy scene in *Romeo and Juliet*. " 'O Tybalt, Tybalt! The best friend I had. That ever I should live to see thee dead! Romeo that killed him, he is banished!' " I laid it on sirloin-thick.

Freddy, back from the dead as Mercutio, predictably whispered, "She said 'breast.' "

" 'No faith, no honesty in men,' " I bellowed. " 'All perjured, all forsworn, all naught. Sorrow makes me old.'" As I read, as I overacted the Nurse's sorrow, my own was lifting. It'd been a day since Noel and I walked to school together. I'd been processing and replaying the conversation for twenty-four hours straight.

Even though hardly anything was said, it had been a good talk.

Matilda Rossi as Juliet recited, " 'I, a maid, die maiden-widowed. I'll to my wedding bed. And death, not Romeo, take my maidenhead!'" She dropped her book and looked directly at Freddy Pluto. "Well, Freddy? I said 'maidenhead.' Aren't you going to comment?"

He squinted, as if he had no clue what she was talking about.

" 'Maidenhead,'" repeated Rossi. "Virginity. Juliet is complaining that Romeo killed her cousin *before* he had a chance to take her to the 'wedding bed' for the first time. She's more bereft with grief over her sexual frustration than her dead cousin. What do you make of that? Freddy?"

He said, "Juliet was a nympho?"

Giggles. Even I laughed. Rossi said, "It means she's fourteen years old! She's a teenager with a one-track mind, who lacks depth of emotion, is completely self-absorbed."

Incidentally, Rossi might be railing against the sexual myopia of teens because of the horrible couple of days she'd had. Although no one was sure what set off the lasagna fight between Vin Transom and Eric Brainard (they weren't divulging), it had been rumored (thanks to Kim Daniels and her SIZE-SIXTEEN MOUTH) that they were having what was euphemistically (and optimistically) referred to as a sword fight over Matilda Rossi.

The brawl over who could be the number one teacher's pet was, according to Ms. Ratzenberger's terse e-mail to students, the first fistfight in Chez Brownstone history. Brownstone had converted from a nunnery to coed secular private K-through-twelve school about a hundred years ago (which would have been an impressive streak to break), but the cafeteria itself had been completely renovated in 2000. Six years without an eruptive incident didn't seem all that impressive. Ratzenberger intended to make examples of "the participants." Without naming the boys, she announced that anyone caught fighting on school property would be suspended for a week. When Vin and Eric didn't appear at school this morning, we knew she'd done her worst.

The word out by the lockers was that Rossi claimed to be the innocent victim of hormonally out-of-control teenage boys with vivid imaginations. Ratzenberger bought it, hook, line and stinker. But Rossi's excuses would get harder and harder to make, I thought, while listening to her wax poetic about the self-absorption of teenage girls.

A knock on the classroom door.

Rossi bid welcome. Then Ms. Ratzenberger, as if she could read and heed my thoughts, entered the room. She said, "Just here to observe," and tippy-toed to a desk as if everyone didn't see and hear her. She picked an empty chair right next to, ahem, me.

The blond ex-model current substitute victim of hormonal teens faked a smile, and said, "Okay, class, on to act three, scene three. Romeo. Friar Laurance."

I raised my hand. Liza gasped, since she knew all about Rossi's odious warning. Noel frowned at me as well. I smiled at him—what I hoped was a *friendly* smile.

Matilda Rossi's blue eyes blazed when she saw my dancing fingers in the air. She didn't call on me. I started waving my arm. I used my other arm to hold it up. Then I flapped both arms, one after the other, as if I were doing the wave with myself.

Ms. Ratzenberger said, "I believe a pupil has a question, Ms. Rossi."

Rossi sighed. "You'd like to excuse yourself to the ladies' room, Ms. Benet?"

"I have a comment on your interpretation of the last scene. The one where Juliet cried to Nurse about how Romeo isn't going to plunder her virginity?"

Ms. Ratzenberger inhaled sharply. I went on. "You said Juliet is this horny teenage girl who is a sex-obsessed slut. Right?"

Rossi said, "I don't believe I phrased it so colorfully."

Ms. Ratzenberger said, "I should hope NOT!"

I said, "I don't believe this scene is about sex. It's about love."

"That's very astute," said Rossi. "Now, class, on to act three, scene three."

I kept talking. "Juliet calls herself a maiden-widow. A virgin wife. She's already committed her heart and soul to Romeo. And, who among us wouldn't grieve more for a spouse than a cousin? When she says 'death take my maidenhead,' Juliet means she's prepared to die a virgin if she can't be with Romeo. That doesn't seem selfish to me. Her virginity is all she has to give to another person in the world. It's quite a lot, actually. And she wants to give herself to Romeo. For her, sex isn't lust. It's loyalty and love."

"Excellent point, Dora," said Ms. Ratzenberger, who might be a virgin herself, for all I knew.

Rossi, from the look of things, was wishing I'd die a virgin, right then and there, at my desk. She said, "Okay. Romeo, start reading from the top of page eighty. 'What less than doomsday . . .' "

Noel said, "I have a comment on Dora's comment."

"Oh, God," said Rossi.

"Romeo is as committed to Juliet as she is to him," he said. "Even though he wants to be with Juliet desperately, he doesn't think of sex with her as a physical act. It would be a blending of souls, which isn't something he's ever done before, so, in a way, they're both virgins. He has no expectations about what would happen. But he would want Juliet to have a good time. In fact, Romeo would probably say that his fun *is* Juliet's fun."

No one spoke for a second. Noel and I didn't dare look at each other.

"Glad we cleared that up," said Rossi.

"I'm not sure we did," said Ms. Ratzenberger.

"Romeo," snapped Rossi. "Doomsday, please."

Twenty-seven

"You summoned me?" I asked Sondra Fortune in the back room at Monty's. She had a large Diet Coke in front of her and a few garlic knots on a plate. On either side of her sat Lori and Micha Dropov. Both of the evil twins were shooting happy daggers at me with their eyes, willing me stabbed, shot, molecularly dematerialized.

Like I didn't want to be beamed out of there? Sondra had called me on my cell exactly ten seconds after school was dismissed for the day. I could have refused to meet her. I could also play in traffic or jump in front of a subway train.

Sondra said, "Fringe! I'm so glad you could stop by. I really appreciate it, and I know how busy you've been lately."

"No inconvenience at all, Sondra," I said. "It's an honor and privilege to be in your presence. And might I add that you look even more beautiful today than you did the last time I saw you, whenever that was."

We smiled at each other, batting eyelashes, seemingly sincere. If a mini Martian had landed on her table at that second, exited her spacecraft and surveyed the scene, she would have reported back to her home planet that earthlings were friendly, generous, loving creatures that only wished health and happiness for each other. And then Sondra would have squashed the tiny alien under her friendly, generous thumb.

She said, "You are too, too kind, Fringe. Love your tan, by the way." She turned her glorious head to the left and right. "Guys, if you don't mind, Fringe Girl has some embarrassing private matters to discuss with me. She's way too mortified to speak to a group."

Lori and Micha grumbled. They hated leaving their seats in the radius of Sondra's power. The twins knew full well that Sondra had called me here. That the embarrassing private matters to discuss were Sondra's. But we all pretended, like good little minions, that the humiliation was mine, all mine. As the Dropovs walked around me on their way out of the back room, Lori stepped on my clog, hard. The anorexic ballet addict was stronger than she looked.

I didn't wait for an invitation to sit down and take a garlic knot. Perhaps bad breath would keep Sondra at arm's length, in the metaphorical sense.

Sondra said, "Help yourself."

"I will."

"You might have forgotten, Fringe, that you were supposed

to be helping me," she snapped suddenly. "I wanted Rossi kicked out of school. Not Vin Transom!"

"I had nothing to do with that fight," I said. "Except supplying the meat-based weaponry."

"If you'd done your job and gotten rid of Rossi, the fight never would've happened. I asked you, as a personal favor to me, to figure out a way to get rid of that woman. You had a vested interest!"

I nodded and chewed. I could do both at the same time. "Rossi is going to get herself kicked out. Sometimes, the path of true wisdom is to stand back, let events unfold, allow things to reach their natural conclusion—"

"Shut up," said Sondra sharply. "This is the last time I come to you—*you!*—for help. You squandered your chance to get in my good graces. You betrayed me. Because of you, Rossi scrambled Vin Transom's head. Because of you, he's been suspended for a week."

Obviously, I had nothing to do with any of it. I certainly played no part in Sondra and Vin's breakup (which was something I couldn't say for her, regarding my split with him several months ago). I gazed at her large emerald eyes, flashing with misplaced anger. I registered the rage underneath her perfect skin—the tan that would never fade. She'd confessed to me in October, in the basement bathroom at Brownstone, the source of her perpetual anger, the heat and scrutiny that fired her craving for power. I alone understood the internal battle Sondra waged against racism, even in the Brownstone community of "tolerance" and "diversity." After all, you could lead a horse to the trough of tolerance. But you couldn't make it drink the Snapple.

"Blame me," I said. "It's okay. I want you to. Maybe that's the only way I can help you."

"I do blame you," she said.

"Good," I said. "I admit that I should have done more for you. I should have put my own problems on hold so that I could devote my time and energy to yours. I didn't. I screwed up. I'm sorry. And if it's any consolation, you can crush me under your thumb like a mini Martian."

I closed my eyes and braced for the squashing. But nothing happened. I opened one eye, and then the other, and beheld a sight I'd never thought I would see.

Sondra was crying.

I was baffled. I was stymied. At a complete loss for how to react to the show of humanity. I stood up. I sat down. I would have turned around three times, patted my head and rubbed my belly if that would have made her stop. Instead, I reached out and covered her hand with mine, only to be poked in the palm by one of her flashy, trashy (in a good way) rings.

"I miss him," she blurted.

I knew firsthand (lip?) that Vin Transom was an excellent kisser. That was the extent of my close encounters with him, apart from random groping. I had to assume that Sondra had done more, and that Vin's fine marathoner body had gone the distance in bed. Besides his sexual allure, Vin stood out in another way for Sondra. He was the only boy she'd been with who'd rejected her. As my parents wrote in *His-and-Her Divorce*, you never loved a man more than when he was walking out the door.

I, of course, had an encyclopedic knowledge of not getting what I wanted. Whereas I'd cultivated a cynical optimism and a wry sense of humor to compensate, Sondra had no idea what to make of her first rejection. Anger was her fallback reaction. But being pissed off at me hadn't made her pain go away.

"I have a suggestion," I said, once she'd stopped sniveling.

She shook her head. "I'm pretty set on blaming you."

"As an alternative—or in addition—you could try apologizing to Vin."

"Oh, for Christ's sake, Fringe Girl," she said, slamming the table with her fist. "I've already tried that. I begged him to take me back. I went to his house and cried and said 'please.' He won't have me. He said he was tired of me."

"Bastard!" I said. Vin Transom, the star tracklete who ran his competition into the ground, the boy who rose at dawn to sprint over the Brooklyn Bridge—this guy got *tired*?

"I hope your groveling embarrassed the hell out of him."

"Him more than me," she said, smiling thinly. "At least I learned how low I could sink."

"The limbo dance of heartbreak," I said.

"I heard you and Noel are talking," she said.

"We're grunting words and sentences in each other's direction at school," I said. "He's not calling, e-mailing, IMing, texting or paging me at home. Our friendship—which is all it is, or is ever going to be—is academic."

She stared into her Diet Coke, but she wouldn't find solace there. I knew. I'd tried.

"Lori and Micha are worried that you've turned on them," I said. "They blame me, too—a hot new trend?"

Sondra laughed. "I'll make it up to them," she said.

"I'll try to make it up to you," I said.

Twenty-eight

Dear Gloria and Ed:

I love my boyfriend, but he's an alcoholic. And when he drinks a lot, he doesn't know what he's doing. He's pushed me around a few times. Once, I hit my head on the edge of the coffee table and had to get stitches. I'm not some idiot who blames herself. I know it's his fault. But he's such a gentle soul when he's sober. My question to you is, How can I make him stop drinking?

                    Desperate in Bensonhurst

Dear Gloria and Ed:

My wife was just diagnosed with breast

cancer. It's early, stage one, and the doctors are optimistic she'll make a full recovery. But she'll have to have a mastectomy. I feel terrible for her and what she has to go through. But I'm worried I'll be disgusted by the change in her body. It's awful to admit. Can you help me get my head on straight?

Hating Myself in Great Neck

Dear Gloria and Ed:

My husband wants me to do a sex act that I find offensive. It would go against my Christian morals. If I don't do it, he says he's going to find someone who will. Do I give up my morals and do what he wants, or hold my ground and watch my marriage fall apart?

Conflicted in Canarsie

Dear Gloria and Ed:

I'm a fourteen-year-old girl. My next-door neighbor locked me in his garage yesterday and molested me. He said if I told anyone, he'd run over my dog. I've been keeping my dog in the house to protect her, but she wants to go out, and she's had a few accidents. My mom is angry at me about

```
it. I haven't gone out myself, except to
school and back to my room. My mom wants to
know what's wrong. She suspects something.
Should I tell her?
                    Scared in Riverdale
```

And those were the first four e-mails I read today. Alcoholism, cancer, perversion and molestation, right off the bat. I did a quick scan of the other two dozen e-mails waiting for a reply. Heartache, betrayal, seduction, lies, cheating. Where were the questions about "Should I wait until the third date to get intimate?" and "If he doesn't call me, can I call him?" Their column was a lot more serious than I'd thought.

Granted, out of fear that they'd write about their sex lives, I'd avoided reading it. I hated their cutesy photo, too. I'd flipped through their books. The content was light (except in *His-and-Her Divorce*, where they'd included a lot of legal stuff). *His-and-Her Romance*, the work in progress, was promising to be lighter than the weight of a thousand angels dancing on the head of Paris Hilton.

But these e-mails. They were heavy. Weighty and depressing. Real people, in real life, in real places, writing to my parents, hoping that two strangers in the posh idyllic wonderland of Brooklyn Heights were going to give them answers to their impossible problems. How desperate did you have to be to think a letter in a newspaper from my parents (who still reminisced about Grateful Dead concerts) could begin to, for instance, help Hating Myself in Great Neck get a grip about his wife's mastectomy? This guy needed serious counseling at Sloan-Kettering or somewhere professional. And the girl who got molested by her neighbor? Why doesn't she go to the police? Hadn't she been taught at school how to handle this? The girlfriend of the drunk brute? Didn't she know that you couldn't stop someone from being an alcoholic?

Dad poked his head into the office, which was a small alcove, known in Brooklyn real estate parlance as a "pocket room" with a sliding door. He asked, "How's it going?"

I said, "What is wrong with these people?"

He walked in, read some of the e-mails over my shoulder. "Well, this woman is battered," he said. "This man's wife has cancer. The religious woman is facing a crisis of conscience. And this girl has been abused."

"I know that!" I said. "Why don't they know what to do? Why are they coming to you and Mom for advice? It's ridiculous."

Dad pursed his lips and sat down next to me in the empty twin purple Lucite swivel desk chair. "You know what problem all of these people share?" he asked. "The problem that's bigger than what they've written to us about?"

"They're uninformed," I said.

He nodded. "True. Chances are, these people don't read *Psychology Today* or the *New York Times*. They didn't go to a private school that includes a curriculum on personal safety, with psychologists on staff to advise students and families at every emotional turn. They don't have doctors and therapists among their family or friends."

"So there's a bigger problem than being uneducated?"

Dad looked at me with seriousness. "They're alone," he said. "Each one of these people is tormented by a shame they can't share. They have no one to confide in, and no one to trust."

"Oh," I said, feeling shame myself, for the compassion I lacked. "I get it."

"Do you, Dora? Do you have any idea how lucky you are? Not only are you well informed, you live in a secure home. You have friends in abundance, a loving family, tremendous resources at Brownstone. You are being watched, cared for, supported, every step of the way by intelligent and compassionate adults."

"Okay, Dad, I get the picture."

"I don't think you do," he said, getting worked up. "All we try to do, your mom and I, is figure out ways to make life easier for you and Joya. That's why we're having your sister tested for ADHD, for one thing. That's why we tolerate the drama from you. And, for all we do to help you, you already have it as easy as any kid on the entire planet! Despite that FACT, you, Dora, run away to Bermuda with stolen money—to a man who'd abandoned his children. Joya locks herself in her room and won't talk to us."

"Can we leave Joya out of it?" I asked. "This is my father-daughter moment. She can have her own scene."

"You accused me of sneaking around behind your mother's back," he said, shaking his head. "I'd asked Patty to come over when Gloria wasn't home so I could surprise her with the money later. You ruined *my* moment."

"I'm sorry, Dad," I said. "I was temporarily insane that day."

He sighed. "Anything you want to talk about? I won't judge."

"Why do you do this?" I asked, tapping the monitor. "Doesn't the pileup of other people's misery get you down?"

"As unbelievable as it might seem to you, Dora, your mom and I write the *Moon* column because we want to *help* people, to whatever extent we can. And helping people makes us feel good."

"For the sweet love of God, Dad," I said. "You're *earnest.*"

"No, Dora," he said, grinning goofy. "I'm Edward."

He left me to my toils. I searched my parents' exhaustive archives and found that they'd written responses already for most of the questions that had come in. I kept at it, sending replies to dozens of lonely people, until dinner.

Everything I'd been philosophizing about, all that new-perspective stuff, had been off. Yes, you could look at the stars and feel insignificant. You could gaze at the sea to make your problems seem small. But when you dove into the truly vast ocean of human heartache—when *I* dove into it—I realized on a tiny molecular level (as in, within each cell in my body) that my own problems *were* small. They just seemed big. In the grand scheme of human struggle, even the minor scheme on this block in Brooklyn Heights, I had nothing to worry about. And if I were really going to meditate on the significance of human existence, what I could glean from my parents was that it began and ended with one's willingness and ability to help.

Shit! I felt it coming on, like a fast-moving flu, a wellspring of earnestness in my own heart. I would have to be very, very careful to keep that caged. At least in public. Or I could disguise it by pouring a gallon of cynicism on top.

My cell phone chirped, saving me from spiraling uncontrollably into a fit of love for my dad, pity for Mrs. Strombone, and the certainty that, if Romeo and Juliet had written an advice column for the *Verona Gazette*, they might have realized that there was life after doomed love.

"Marry," I said, answering the phone.

"Pardon?" asked the man on the other end.

"Yes, hello." I checked caller ID. A number with a 603 area code. New Hampshire?

"Is Dora Benet available?"

"You don't know how much," I said.

"She called me a week or so ago, regarding a former employee of mine. A Matilda Rossi?"

"Are you from Exeter?"

"Yes, I'm the director of faculty at the school."

"Mr. Bingley," I said, remembering his name. "Thanks for returning my call."

"How may I help you?"

Down to business. "I'm checking references on Ms. Rossi," I said, deepening my voice, trying to sound official.

"You said you're with the Brownstone Collegiate Institute in Brooklyn, New York?"

"That's right."

"We've already sent a packet on Ms. Rossi to Ms. Velma Ratzenberger. About three months ago."

Velma??? "I'm just following up on some details," I said, trying to sound official. "Ms. Ratzenberger is my boss. Why did Ms. Rossi leave her job at Exeter?"

He paused. "I'm sorry, I'm not at liberty to discuss that."

"Did she get involved with a student?" I asked, my (earnest) heart doing jumping jacks in my chest.

"Good golly, no!" he said. "We didn't suggest anything like that in the material we sent to Ms. Ratzenberger. As per our agreement with Ms. Rossi, the reason she left is confidential."

"Yes, I see that in the file," I said, flipping magazine pages. "But you are at liberty to say whether her offense was criminal." I had no idea what I was saying. But it was worth a try.

"We discovered that she'd been using school property for nonacademic purposes, which is a violation of our charter, but not a criminal act."

So she *was* fired. "That depends on how she was using the property. If she was using her office to sell stolen jewelry, as we suspect . . ."

"She didn't do that!" he said. "Nothing like that!" And then, to my amazement, he told me the truth. He'd wanted to, badly. I could hear the anger in his tone when he described what Rossi had done with Exeter letterhead and on the school computers.

We hung up. He was glad to have ratted her out, although I was sworn to secrecy.

Naturally, I'd crossed my fingers. As a secularist, the only swearing I did was the dirty kind.

Speaking of which, I had the grade-A *shit* on Matilda Rossi. And I knew just how to fling it.

Twenty-nine

"I'd like to propose," said Ryan Greene, "a toast."

It was a frigid Saturday. The wedding was only days away, on Tuesday evening. An odd night for a wedding. But, as I've established, Stephanie Greene was sentimental (emphasis on "mental"), and she insisted her second wedding would take place on Valentine's Day, the trumped-up phony holiday hated by singles the world over, especially me. But, then again, not having a boyfriend, even on V-Day, was not a tragedy.

The rehearsal dinner, where no one rehearsed or had a full dinner, was at the River Café, the fancy-schmantzy Frenchy restaurant that was actually a floating barge on the East River. It was three o'clock in the afternoon, but that was the only time Stephanie could secure, since we weren't going to have the famous tasting menu of twelve courses for three hundred dollars per person. The bride had had to settle for half a dozen plates of hors d'oeuvres and champagne cocktails for twenty. And that meager bounty would cost more than the home wedding three days hence.

At a round table, Liza sat to my right, Eli to my left. Stanley Nable sat to Liza's right. They could have shared a chair. She was squeezed so close to him, she might as well have been on top of him.

I asked her, "How does Ryan like the Brooklyn Marriott?"

"He likes it so much he's decided to stay awhile," said Liza with a wink.

"You stole his passport?" asked Eli, munching on a triangle of smoked salmon on toast.

"I didn't have to," said Liza. "Although that was my Plan B."

"What was Plan A?" asked Eli.

"To get my parents in the same room and let the old black magic take over."

Joya, seated next to Eli, said, "I love that plan!"

"It's working," whispered Liza, beaming, bursting with love from every pore, which was how I liked her.

Stanley liked her that way, too, and kissed her on the cheek.

Across the room, Gary Glitch, seated with Stephanie and his parents, frowned aggressively at Ryan, who was getting nattier by the day. The New Yorker in him was reemerging, and he looked downright dapper in a Hugo Boss suit.

I said, "Gary seems thrilled to have Ryan as a wedding guest."

"Check out his parents."

The elder Glitches, flown in from Ohio, were wearing red turtlenecks (which we all found appropriate). They had been, in their prime, state polka champions. Pushing seventy, their dancing days behind them, they'd apparently given up on conversation, too, staying in their corner, not speaking or smiling. I felt a pang of sympathy for Gary. Having prunes for parents couldn't have been fun. Then again, they probably kept him regular.

Liza's grandparents hadn't arrived yet. They were expected in time for the wedding. Liza suspected they were staging a passive protest, since they'd always loved Ryan. Matt Greene, also at the table of death, sat next to his mother. He was sulking, ignoring me with such volcanic force that I feared he'd explode.

"Should I apologize to Matt?" I asked.

Stanley's ears pricked up. He asked, "What did you do to him?"

I shook my head and said, "It's personal."

"Okay."

"Really, none of your business," I said adamantly.

"Sorry I asked."

"Jesus, you just won't let it go! Fine, I'll tell you. I turned him down flat. Absolutely nothing happened between us."

Stanley said, "Interesting news. If you ladies will excuse me, I have a phone call to make." He flipped open his cell and pretended to dial. "Hello, *Noel*?" he said into it, grinning.

I said, "Like you're not going to tell him everything."

Stanley said, "You know you want me to."

I leaned across the table and made a grab for his phone. He whisked it away, laughing.

Liza said, "God, I'm glad we made up," and kissed him. Gary looked over at us. His face turned white when he saw their lip-lock.

Ryan cleared his throat. "I know it might seem odd to have a first husband at the rehearsal dinner for the second marriage," he said. "First of all, thank you, Stephanie, for letting me be here."

Stephanie said, "Your invitation is in the mail."

Everyone laughed politely. Stephanie and Ryan locked eyes.

"They've been doing that for days," whispered Liza excitedly.

Joya said, "I can see the energy between them. It's visible."

I groaned, but Liza was nodding at my sister. "I see it, too!"

"It's purple," said Joya. "And glittery."

"Exactly!" said Liza.

Eli and I looked at each other and shrugged. Visions were beyond us. We were earthbound. Eli was the earth, and Liza was the sun. They went together, influenced each other. Were in balance.

Joya, eyes twinkling, smiled at me beautifully, warmly, giddy on her rainbow dreams for someone else's happiness. She was my balance, my moon, orbiting around me, secretly, silently keeping my tides, my days and nights. Taking no credit where it was way overdue.

"Oh, shit," I said, tearing up.

Eli said, "What is wrong with you now?"

"I'm feeling the love."

"Fingers crossed," said Liza.

"And legs," I said. To Stanley: "Which you can also tell Noel."

Ryan continued. "I was married to Stephanie for twenty wonderful years. We had two beautiful children, Matt and Liza. We made so many great friends—including the Stomps and the Benets, who are all here tonight. I'm grateful for those years, Stephanie. I've got regrets, too."

"He does?" I asked Liza.

"He better!" she said.

Ryan went on. "As most of you know, I've been living in a beach house in Bermuda for the last three years. I moved to the island because I was worn out by the New York pace. I felt like I'd been running for twenty years. I honestly believed I would run myself to death if I stayed. I needed to slow down. And so I have. Except for missing my family, and my regrets about leaving the way I did, I've been happy. That's what I wish for you, Stephanie," he said. "I want you to be happy. Living alone on an island has taught me a lot about our marriage. I never gave you enough credit for all you did to make me happy, even though I doubt I could have ever been the man you deserved in this environment. But you tried, all along, which is far, far more than I can say for myself. If I could change anything about my life thus far, I would have been a more considerate, compassionate husband. You deserved that. And I'm sorry I let you down."

Stephanie Greene, for once, was dry-eyed. She gaped at Ryan, as we all did.

Eli whispered, "Not a traditional rehearsal dinner toast, but effective nonetheless."

Liza, meanwhile, had died and gone to *Parent Trap* heaven. She stood up, raised her glass, and said, "What Dad means to say is, 'Here's to Stephanie. The woman he never stopped loving.' "

"Cheers!" rejoiced the group, with the exception of Stephanie, who'd been stunned silent by the apology she'd waited years to hear, and Gary, who would have wrung Ryan's suntanned neck if he could have reached that far across the table. Gary's polka parents hadn't the first clue what was really going on, but they didn't seem to care anyway.

Ryan emptied his flute of champagne in one gulp. "And now that I've said too much and had too much to drink, I'll excuse myself," he said. "I'll be at the Marriott, in case anyone needs to find me."

Matt Greene jumped up and followed his father out. Liza, too, ran after her father and brother. From where I was sitting, I could see the three of them standing in a huddle on the ramp that connected the floating restaurant to land. The fractured family, pieced back together. Matt seemed flustered and upset. He'd tried to emulate what he thought had been his father's detachment, his isolation by choice. Although he'd gone to live on one, Ryan Greene was not an island. I wondered if Matt's next girlfriend would be more than someone he enjoyed spending time with, and whether sex with her would go beyond a physical act.

"I can't imagine how the next toast could top that one," said Eli. "So I might as well leave."

Stanley, who could also see the Greenes on the ramp from his seat, knew he'd get no more attention from Liza today. He said, "I'll take you." He had a Vespa.

Eli waved to her parents and left with Stanley. They convened with the Greene trio on the way out. I was pleased to see Ryan give Stanley a rib-crushing hug, a damn-glad-to-meet-you two-handed shake, a manic slap on the back.

Joya was also watching the love-in.

I said, "Ryan just wants everyone to be happy."

Joya said, "Is that comment earnest, or cynical?"

"Both?" I asked.

"You can't have it both ways, Dora."

"I can try," I said.

The toasting had stopped in the aftermath of Ryan's exit. If anyone was waiting for Liza and Matt to come back, we'd be here all night. The three Greenes had already left, along with Eli and Stanley. I assumed they were off to the Marriott, Brooklyn Heights's finest (and only) hotel.

Stephanie had recovered use of her eyelids and jaw. She was listening to Gary Glitch whisper frantically in her ear. Joya asked, "What do you think he's saying?"

I channeled Gary and said, " 'Your family hates me, and they've ruined our night.' "

Joya spoke for Stephanie, whose lips were now moving. " 'They're my children. Love them or leave me.' "

" 'If that's what you want.' " I replied for Gary.

" 'That's how it is, buster.' " Joya answered for Stephanie.

And then Gary pushed back his chair. He barked something terse to his parents. Then the three of them got up and stormed out of the restaurant.

Joya put her fingers over her mouth. "Oh my God!" she said. "Did we do that?"

"I wonder if it's a nonrefundable deposit on the Ossining house."

Mom had been watching the betrothed couple, too. As soon as Gary cleared the area, she rushed to Stephanie's side. Dad stopped at the bar to get a stiff drink for the bride (ex-bride? late bride? once-and-former bride?) and then took the seat at her other side. They sandwiched her. They were two slices of wholesome, multigrain sympathetic bread. Stephanie was their raw, red meat.

Anita and Bertram Stomp sat down at our table. Anita said, "I never liked Ryan Greene. Until five minutes ago."

Bertram asked, "What was his house like, Dora? The Bermuda place?"

"It was amazing," I lied for no reason. "Right on the beach."

Anita mulled that over. "He gave a lovely speech. But he won't give up his lifestyle. Stephanie and Ryan are right back where they were four years ago. It's a hopeless impasse."

"If only we could think of an outside-the-box solution," I said. "Hey, isn't that your specialty, Anita? Amicable settlements?"

"Yes," said Bertram, nodding. "It is."

Joya, Bertram and I smiled at Anita, the ball-breaking

lawyer, who was famous for her "win–win" negotiation style. She stared at us, until, slowly, a loose smile crept across her usually tight face.

"I've got an idea," said Anita, "that might fix all of their wagons."

Thirty

A Brooklyn Winter's Tale
Week VI, Scene I
English lit class, Monday morning

"'You green-sickness carrion! You tallow-face!'" read Stanley as Lord Capulet, Juliet's father. "'You baggage! Disobedient wretch!'"

My thoughts exactly, regarding Matilda Rossi. As Juliet, she begged for her father's forgiveness. Juliet had the sass to refuse to marry Paris, the local hottie man of wax.

Stanley read on. "'We thought us blest that God had let us this only child. But now I see this one is one too much. And that we have a curse in having her.'"

I, Nurse, read my lines of protest, defending Juliet.

Stanley read, " 'God's bread!' "

Freddy mumbled, "He said . . ."

Ms. Rossi said, "He said 'bread,' Freddy. 'Bread.' The food. Okay, Lord Capulet. You're telling Juliet that if she doesn't marry the man you picked for her, you're going to throw her out. Go on, Stanley."

" 'Hang, beg, starve, die on the street,' " he recited.

"Harsh," said Freddy.

Ms. Ratzenberger, observing, was seated next to me again. Behind Noel, in front of Liza and Stanley. The administrator had been barely paying attention and was filling out forms at her desk.

Rossi as Juliet read, " 'O sweet Mother, cast me not away! Delay this marriage for a month, a week.' "

Liza as Lady Capulet read, " 'Talk not to me, for I'll not speak a word. Do as thou wilt, for I am done with thee.' "

Juliet has a whiny BREAST-beating monologue. And then I get to deliver my last speech of the play, my final shining moment. And it's a wimpy one. I read, " 'I think it best you marry Paris. He's a lovely gentleman! Romeo hath not so green, so quick, so fair an eye as Paris hath.' "

It was Nurse's last gust of influence on Juliet. For all the skulking around she did on behalf of the star-crossed lovers, when the time came for her to put her own life of luxury on the line (if Juliet were kicked out of the manor, Nurse would have to go with her), the withered, widowed woman would rather Juliet betray her heart and suck up to her wretched parents. With that one bit of bad advice, Nurse taught Juliet the sad truth, that she was alone in the world now, except for Romeo.

Rossi said, "What's happening in this scene? Liza? Perhaps you'd like to offer something for once?"

The snide tone made Ms. Ratzenberger look up over her glasses, but briefly.

Liza said, "Juliet's parents are ganging up on her to push her into a marriage she doesn't want."

"What do you make of the Capulet marriage?" asked Ms. Rossi.

"It's not a good one," said Liza. "Lord Capulet is mean. And Lady Capulet is too afraid of him to stand up for herself, or for Juliet."

"How does that affect Juliet?"

Liza paused to think. "Juliet is the product of a bad marriage. Probably, in fourteenth-century Verona, people didn't get divorced. Nowadays, Juliet would be a child of divorce. And maybe her parents wouldn't be so horrible to her if they were split up. As much as a child wants her parents to stay married and to live as a family, it's probably better for each parent to be happy in their separate lives. It's not an ideal world. Sometimes, even if two people love each other, they can't be together for practical reasons. And that's sad. But their kids can make peace with it. If the parents have made peace with it."

Stanley waved his arm in the air. Rossi pointed at him. He said, "Just to add to Liza's point. Juliet can't be blamed for going a little crazy, given her parents' bad marriage. It could have been even worse for Juliet, if, say, her parents did divorce, and her mother was set to marry another man she didn't really love but thought would provide security for her daughter. Maybe this guy was a racist jerk, too. You would totally understand if Juliet freaked out on her friends. And her friends, especially Romeo, might not know how to handle how upset she is. But if Romeo let her down, he would be very sorry. And he's relieved her mother isn't going to marry that racist idiot after all."

Ms. Ratzenberger looked up at the word "idiot" and then looked back down at her forms.

Liza said, "Juliet is sorry she used Romeo as a pawn."

The reunited lovebirds cooed at each other across the row of desks.

Rossi slammed her copy of *Romeo and Juliet* down on her desk. She said, "First Adora Benet and Noel Kepner, using our classroom discussions to work through their personal lives. And now Liza Greene and Stanley Nable. None of you are paying the least bit of attention to the play, the language, the symbolism. All you want to do is turn it into a reflection of your own overly emotional lives."

Ms. Ratzenberger was now paying attention.

I whispered to Liza, "Who's being overly emotional?"

"I heard that, Ms. Benet. We had an agreement that you'd respect the rules of my classroom, and you've interrupted me yet again. You fail to grasp even the simplest literary concepts, like chiaroscuro and leitmotif. You are, as of right now, failing my class."

Ms. Ratzenberger said, "What's going on?"

I stood up. "I'll tell you what's going on," I said. "Ms. Rossi doesn't want us to form original ideas inspired by the source material. She's anti-interpretation, which is not very Brownstone." I drew breath. "Ms. Ratzenberger, there's something else you need to know about Matilda Rossi."

"Sit *down*, Benet!" warned Rossi.

"That woman," I said, pointing at the fuming blond substitute, "is a REPUBLICAN!"

"What?" asked Ms. Ratzenberger.

"Not only is she a Republican," I said, "In 2002, when she was at Exeter, she used school property—letterhead, computers, mailing lists— to CAMPAIGN FOR THE REELECTION OF GEORGE BUSH. And she's pushing her right-wing agenda again! Right here at Brownstone." I turned toward Rossi. "It was that joke I told on the second day. About Bush and the Brazilian soldiers. You've been gunning for me ever since."

Ms. Ratzenberger's face turned white as chalk. "Is this true, Matilda?"

Rossi didn't look quite as beautiful when her face was crunched with anger. For a scary half second, I thought she might lunge at me. She said, "It's my calling—and my challenge—to teach the future leaders of America, to present thoughts, ideas and concepts. A biased or one-sided interpretation of literature— or the current political climate—is limiting intellectually."

"You made Eric Brainard publish that prowar editorial in the *Brief* and start a Young Republicans club," I said.

"I merely educated him about neocon philosophy and political science," she said. "He made his own decisions."

Noel Kepner stood up. "She asked me to go to a Bill O'Reilly book reading with her. When you walked in on us, Dora. She got on her knees and pleaded. I thought she was coming on to me. But she was really trying to convert me."

Under her breath, Rossi muttered, "Another Jew who thinks he knows everything."

A roomful of faces dropped in shock. Rossi's beautiful (but malevolent) eyes widened. She put her hand over her mouth, as if she hadn't intended to speak aloud. But she had, and everyone had heard.

Including Ms. Ratzenberger. Her eyes bulged. She made a garbled sound, clutched her chest, and keeled over.

I screamed, "Strombone!"

Twenty cell phones dialed 911 en masse. A few kids ran out to get the school nurse. I kept my eyes on Rossi. She gathered her purse, some papers, and slipped out the door.

Before she left, she looked right at me. I waved good-bye.

She gave me the finger.

Week VI, Scene II
The Greene family living room, Tuesday evening, Valentine's Day

"Here slums the bride," I said to Eli. We sat next to each other on the floor.

"You can't blame Stephanie for that," said Eli.

Marry, I couldn't. It wasn't her fault that Gary, in his snit about being jilted (he'd been *such* a bad sport about it), canceled the caterer, the table and chair rental, the flowers, the tux rentals. What he couldn't cancel—the gown, the bridesmaid dresses, the cake, the food—he had the tailor and caterer send to his own apartment in Manhattan. He'd be eating prime rib and crudités until spring. In taffeta.

I almost felt sorry for him. Almost.

Liza walked up the makeshift aisle, aka the space between the dozen-odd people sitting Indian style on the carpet to the right and those on the left. She wore a simple cream silk sheath that showed off her curves. She sprinkled rose petals as she walked, and threw a heaping handful at Eli and me as she passed. Jack Carp, Eli's "not date," played the Wagner piece on his portable digital keyboard. Bertram Stomp, a hidden talent, accompanied on kazoo.

Stephanie was wearing a blue suit, a loaner from my mom. Gloria had worn the Chanel number one too many times for TV interviews and had retired it from public use. She was glad to give it to Stephanie, who, although as slim as Gloria, was much taller. The dignified length on Gloria was a lot shorter on Stephanie, transforming a staid suit into a sexy one.

From our seats on the floor, the skirt was, perhaps, too sexy. We could look up and see more thigh than was appropriate for a PG-13 event. Stephanie's father walked alongside her and blocked our view. I was grateful to him. I might thank him later.

At the top of the "aisle," Stephanie's father kissed her, handed her off to the groom, kissed Liza, kissed Matt (who smiled sweetly) and sat on the couch next to his wife.

Matt, in jeans and a crisp white shirt, looked not only

handsome but happy. I was glad for him and what all this might mean for his philosophical views. That said, I wasn't going within fifty feet of the guy.

Anita Stomp, standing between the bride and the groom, said, "We're all here. Everyone in place. Let's begin." Along with being a lawyer, Anita was also a certified and elected justice of the peace, Kings County, Borough of Brooklyn, City of New York. When Gary canceled the priest, Anita Stomp stepped up.

"We've been here before," Anita said, and everyone laughed. "You agree and accept the terms we've negotiated, and the binding contracts we signed this morning?"

Stephanie nodded. "I willingly agree to move to Bermuda and be the accountant and promotional supervisor for Greene Snorkel Tours."

Ryan said, "And I willfully agree to spend the months of December, January and February in Brooklyn. Sublet an apartment. See some shows. Go to museums." He winked at Matt.

Anita said, "And I—speaking on behalf of myself, my husband and my daughter—are thrilled to welcome Liza into our home, to feed her and make sure she does her homework, until she graduates from Brownstone in June of next year. We talked about escorting her to Bermuda for vacations. But I think we all know Liza can find her way down there by herself."

Some laughs from the crowd. Mom, Dad and Joya, seated one row up, glanced back at me in unison and smiled.

Lump in throat. I tried to swallow it, but it was stuck. I

looked to my right, for some of Eli's stoical stability, but she was grinning and crying and catching rolling tears with her tongue (which was both touching and gross). Liza had already moved most of her clothes into the Stomps' guest bedroom. Eli was finally getting what she'd always wanted, or as close to a real sibling as she could hope to get.

"Second time's the charm," said Anita. "Stephanie, do you take Ryan for your husband?"

"I do," said Stephanie.

"Ryan, do you take Stephanie for your wife?"

"I never stopped," he said.

"I now pronounce you husband and wife. Again."

Applause, cheers, whistles and whoops.

Anita added, "You may now kiss the groom."

Stephanie didn't need to hear that twice. She grabbed Ryan and smooched the snorkel out of him (if you know what I mean). We were totally embarrassed. But it was sweet. Also sick.

Week VI, Scene III
The Benet living room table, Tuesday evening

Mom and Dad sat on the couch. He was massaging her feet. He said, "If the shoes hurt you so much, why do you wear them?"

"Don't be stupid," she said.

Joya and I watched them from the other couch. I said, "Parents, Joya and I have an announcement."

Their heads snapped in our direction. Dad said, "You're going to apologize for being ungrateful beasts to us lately?"

My sister and I looked at each other. Tentatively, I said, "Yyyyesss, if that's a good softener."

"Get on with it," said Mom. She was tired. She'd been serving as Stephanie Greene's round-the-clock sounding board for the last two days.

I said, "Joya and I were inspired by the contract Anita Stomp worked out for Stephanie and Ryan."

"You wrote a contract?" asked Dad, bemused. "Is this some kind of attempt—which will be unsuccessful—to get out of answering e-mails for the column?"

"This contract isn't about me," I said, sliding the paper across the coffee table. "I'm representing Joya."

Dad leaned forward (crushing Mom's legs) and took the page. "It starts well," he said.

AGREEMENT BETWEEN JOYA BENET AND HER WISE AND
BENEVOLENT PARENTS, GLORIA AND EDWARD BENET

1. Joya will, from this day forward, bring home a daily written log of each homework assignment.
2. She will keep a weekly schedule of quizzes and tests.
3. She will submit, weekly, a list of all numerical and letter grades received.
4. She will do her homework immediately after

school, and consider it done only after a parent has scrutinized her work.

5. She will consent to being tested for any learning disability.

6. She will attend tutoring sessions, provided that she chooses the tutor, based on qualification and personality.

IN EXCHANGE . . .

1. The Wise and Benevolent Parents (henceforth W&B Ps) will allow Joya to see Ben Teare three evenings a week, after the above-stated parental approval of homework has been granted.

2. The W&B Ps will, from this day forward, stop attending her classes at Brownstone.

3. The W&B Ps will take Joya's thoughts and feelings into account regarding treatment for any learning disabilities that may or may not be diagnosed in the above-mentioned testing.

4. The W&B Ps will consider whether a specialty art school is worth pursuing for Joya's continuing education. Or maybe art camp, for starters.

5. Should she stay at Brownstone, the W&B Ps will bring Joya to any conferences with school teachers and administrators and never sneak around behind her back again.

6. Finally, the W&B Ps acknowledge that, even

though she is young, her relationship with Ben Teare is of real importance to her and that any attempts to squash it will only make it stronger.

Mom and Dad scanned the agreement with their heads together. They were so used to reading together, they'd adopted the same speed. They finished at the same moment. Before looking at me and Joya, they had a nonverbal exchange with their eyes. Ordinarily, I hated it when they did that little telepathic trick. But, for once, I could understand their unspoken conversation.

Mom said, "We accept your terms. Frankly, we'd probably agree to anything. We're exhausted from all this tension."

Joya jumped up and started clapping her hands as if she'd just won a car on *The Price Is Right*. She leapt over the living room table and hugged the W&B Ps with all the might of her little arms.

I watched. I always watched. I liked to do it, not only because I was good at it. Often, especially now, watching was enough to make me happy.

Thirty-one

"Attendance!" bellowed Mr. Brutowski, the lower school gym teacher who was sitting in for the dismissed Matilda Rossi until Ms. Barbaloo returned (any day now) with a brand-new hip. "Adora Benet!"

"Here," I replied.

Mr. Brutowski looked up. "Where?"

I waved.

He said, "Funny. You don't look like a menace to society."

Word had gotten out about what had happened in class, but a grotesquely distorted version, thanks to the human broadcast network of Kim Daniels.

By the way, Ms. Ratzenberger's coronary was minor, and she was expected to make a full recovery. I was greatly relieved to learn that she had a family history of heart disease.

Elderly women with heart conditions: 0. Dora Benet's questioning of authority: 2.

"Liza Greene!" shouted Mr. Brutowski.

"Hello," she said. To me: "I heard that there's a movement among the middle school boys to start a 'Bring Back Rossi' campaign."

"Stanley Nable!"

"Yo," he replied. To me: "I heard that the first item on their To Do list is to burn you in effigy."

"Just as long as they don't make my dummy look fat," I said.

Yes, I was hated now by nearly the entire male student body, for ridding the school of the one true hottie on the premises. Besides Sondra Fortune, of course. I hadn't heard from her yet. I hoped she was pleased by the way things had played out. Although I was sure she'd find something to blame me for regardless.

"Noel Kepner!" barked Brutowski.

"Sir, yes, sir!" he replied.

I smiled at him. He smiled back.

Progress! I thought.

BUZZZzzzffffsst. The buzzer in our apartment hallway sounded like it'd been smothered in marshmallow, wrapped in plastic and submerged in a bath of Jell-O.

"It works!" shouted Mom into the intercom, her finger on the TALK switch. She toggled back to LISTEN. Dead silence.

Mom said, "Dora, go downstairs and tell her I still can't hear a thing."

I groaned. It was colder than Lady Capulet's teat out there. And the climate inside was so much warmer lately (in so many ways). But I didn't want to give Mom an argument. Especially not while Joya was at the kitchen table in the middle of her tutoring session with Ben Teare, who, along with being her boyfriend and a sharp dresser, was a varsity mathlete.

Grumbling, I piled on my layers and went out to the stoop.

"Mom says she can't hear you," I reported to the visiting electrician who'd volunteered to fix our buzzer for free when she learned it was broken.

"Really?" asked Leslie Strombone, daughter of our bedridden neighbor and chief technician for Fuse Box, her business in Montreal. She ripped the intercom cover off the console.

"Are buzzers different in Canada?" I asked. "Metric, or something?"

She poked at the wires. "This one is just really old. It might be older than I am," she said.

I stood there, waited for her to say more. When she didn't, I said, "Are you mad I lied to you? That day on the phone."

Leslie Strombone, a solid, attractive brunette around Mom's age, said, "I knew you were lying. My mom would never admit she was wrong. And she'd never accept me."

"Still, you and your mom have this great opportunity to forgive and forget, and enjoy the little time you have left together in harmony and love," I said.

Leslie shook her head. "Brooklyn has really changed since I left. When I lived here, people were cynical, not earnest."

"I am cynical!" I said.

She tested the intercom. "Hello? Hello?" No response from Mom upstairs. She said, "It'll never be harmonious with my mother. Look, I came back. I'm helping her. I'm doing my duty. But there are some things you can't forgive." Leslie seemed startled by a thought—not a good one. "I'm a lot more like my mother than I thought."

My mother would try to find a way to forgive, no matter what the circumstances. I hoped I was more like Gloria than I thought.

Leslie screwed the cover back on and toggled the TALK switch. "Gloria? Are you there?" she asked.

Mom was there, all right. And she would always be there for me, until the day she died.

Later that night, Mom and Dad went to a movie. Joya was at Ben's. I was alone on a Friday night. No shame. I was glad about it, to tell the truth. I put on *Mystery Men* for the tenth time, wondering how the Academy of Motion Picture Arts and Sciences failed year after year to recognize the comic genius of Ben Stiller.

My cell chirped.

I said, "Cello."

"Fringe," said Sondra Fortune. "I'm calling to say 'thank you,' and 'you're welcome.'"

"There must be something wrong with my phone. I thought I heard you say 'thank you.'"

"Hold on," she said. "It gets even more incredible. How's this: 'You were right; I was wrong.'"

"Oh, now you've done it. Hell is about to freeze over. Monkeys will soon fly out of my ass."

Sondra laughed—at me, not with me. "Crude bitch," she said.

"What exactly was I right about, if I may so gloat?" I asked.

"You said I shouldn't blame the breakup with Vin on something—someone—outside the relationship. Some things have come to light between us. I won't elaborate, because it's none of your business. But even if I can't blame Rossi—or you—for what went wrong, I'm still pleased she's gone. So, I will repeat only once: 'Thanks.'"

"You said 'you're welcome.' What do I have to thank you for? Besides acknowledging me with your gloriousness, et cetera."

"I said I'd owe you one if you got rid of Rossi. And I kept my promise."

"I don't understand."

"You will," and then she hung up.

Thirty-two

BUZZzzzzfffsst.

The buzzer. It was functioning, barely. I'd only just flipped my phone closed when it sputtered.

I hauled my lazy ass off the couch and slogged to the intercom. I said, "Hello?"

No response.

"Anyone there?"

Nothing but a faint hiss.

So much for Leslie Strombone's Canadian expertise. Well, I was not going to walk all the way downstairs to tell some Jehovah's Witness to peddle his religion somewhere else, so I went over to the kitchen window. Bracing for the frigid blast, I flung it open and leaned outside to see who was on the stoop.

"Hello, down there," I yelled.

A puffy-jacketed figure looked up. He walked down the stoop steps, all the better to see me.

He yelled up, "But soft! What light through yonder window breaks? It is the east, and Dora is the sun. Arise, fair sun and kill the . . . Look, I'm freezing my nads off down here! Lemme in."

I slammed the window shut, and buzzed the door open. So much for our balcony scene.

I waited on our landing for Noel to climb the three flights. Amazingly, I wasn't anxious or jumpy. My heart was slow and steady. My nerves were calm and collected. I was at peace with however this would play out. But I was glad he'd come.

Noel thumped up in his boots. I watched his hand move up the banister, closer and closer to me on the top landing. And then he was standing on it. Five feet away from me.

He said, "Stairs."

"Better than the gym," I said.

"I shouldn't have given you reason to doubt me," he said abruptly. "It all started on the first day back after break, when I put my arm around Sondra. I tried to downplay it. But I should have respected how upset you were. And, I admit, I might have flirted a bit with Rossi. For the record, I did that to impress my friends. They were into her, and she seemed to notice me. It was stupid. I didn't think how you'd feel, even though I knew you were jealous of other girls."

He paused for breath. So far, I'd give his speech an A+. I said, "What about sex?"

"I never wanted to have sex with you."

"Excuse me?" Okay, he was now marked down to an F.

"No, of course I did! I do! Painfully," he blustered. "I mean that I never would have pressured you for it. All those times I invited you over when my parents were out. I really just wanted to be alone with you. And if that included sex, great. Incredible. Dream come true."

"I get it," I said.

"If we didn't do it, a night alone with you would be only slightly less amazing. Honestly, I just wanted to spend as much time with you as possible."

"Anything else?" I asked.

He had to think. "I also should have called you. It was wrong to blow you off that weekend. And it was wrong to go mental on you with that older guy. I know he was just a friend."

"He was. And then he wasn't. For about five minutes," I admitted tersely but warmly.

Noel nodded. He seemed to be thrown by my confession. "I didn't pull the trigger with him," I added. "I didn't even get close to the gun. Never got it out of the holster, if you get my meaning."

"I do," he said.

"Maidenhead intact," I clarified.

"Ridiculously glad to hear it."

"I'm curious," I said. "What made you decide to come over here and say all of this?"

"Don't get mad," he said. "Sondra and I met for coffee at

Grind this afternoon. I know you think she's a snotty, selfish bitch, but she's really insightful about relationships. Anyway, she set me straight about how I'd messed up. And she told me I'd better apologize right away if I harbored any hope of getting back in your good graces."

You're welcome, Sondra, I thought and smiled.

"So?" he asked. "Am I? Back in your good graces?" Noel shuffling in his boots, starting to sweat under his coat/scarf/sweater/gloves.

Let him sweat, I thought.

For two seconds. "Okay," I said. "We can hit rewind. Not a moment too soon, actually. So much has happened in the last month and a half. Not just with you. But with everything. And you were the one I most wanted to talk to about it. So we're going to have to make up for a lot of lost time."

I invited Noel back into my life, my heart, my head, my gut, my soul.

I invited him into another place, too.

The kitchen. For a snack.

If you thought I meant somewhere else, perhaps a particular body part, you really should get your mind out of the gutter.

Marry, perv.

Author's Note

I took one or two liberties with William Shakespeare's *Romeo and Juliet*. Nothing major. Since the play was read aloud in class by my characters, I had to streamline some scenes for my own selfish purposes—namely, narrative flow. I didn't change any of Shakespeare's language. Nor did I move from one scene to the next willy-nilly. I stayed with the scene, line by line, except when I had to skip over a quatrain here and there. Apologies to the Bard.

About the Author

Valerie Frankel is the author of nine previous novels, including *I Take This Man*, *The Accidental Virgin*, *The Girlfriend Curse*, *Hex and the Single Girl* and *Fringe Girl*. She writes often for magazines, including *Self*, *Glamour*, *Marie Claire* and *Allure*. When not working, Val plays Snood, blogs, jogs and takes amateur-quality digital portraits. She lives in Brooklyn Heights with her husband, two daughters and three cats. All of them are extremely photogenic. Go to www.valeriefrankel.com and see for yourself.